The Mental Gymnast

THE DECISION

BOOK ONE
A Vow to Tell the Truth

By Marcia Daigo

*A contemporary, adult, romantic drama
about people who blame everyone but themselves.*

The Mental Gymnastics Trilogy.

The Decision: A Vow to Tell the Truth (Book One) by Marcia Daigo

Copyright © 2017 by Marcia Daigo.

Chief Editor: Wendy Yorke

Editor: Daniella Blechner

All rights reserved. This book or any portion thereof may not be reproduced or used in any manner whatsoever without the express written permission of the publisher except for the use of brief quotations in a book review.

This is a work of fiction. Names, characters, businesses, places, events and incidents are either the products of the author's imagination or used in a fictitious manner. Any resemblance to actual persons, living or dead, or actual events is purely coincidental.

Printed in the United Kingdom

First Printing 2017

Published by Conscious Dreams Publishing

www.consciousdreamspublishing.com

ISBN: 978-1999809171

CONTENTS

Dedication 7
Acknowledgements 9

Chapter one
A Good Catch 11

Chapter two
Tomorrow Is Another Day 31

Chapter three
Putting Temptation in Harm's Way 47

Chapter four
No Freer, Than a Caged Bird 65

Chapter five
Two Shakes of a Cat's Tail 81

Chapter six
The Pressure 101

Chapter seven
The Planning 115

Chapter eight
What Happens Behind Closed Doors... 131

Chapter nine
The Straw That Broke The Camel's Back 141

Chapter ten
It Is Time 159

About the Author 171

DEDICATION

I dedicate this book to my son Akeem, for being there to motivate and selflessly support me when I needed it.

ACKNOWLEDGEMENTS

I would like to acknowledge my mum, Lydia and all the people I know who have encouraged me to write this book. Your confidence in my ability has been invaluable.

I would also like to thank Daniella Blechner, my publisher, Wendy Yorke, my editor, and Oksana Kosovan, my typesetter, whose skills and expertise supported my vision to become a published author.

CHAPTER ONE

A Good Catch

Time: 6am; 4 hours 00 minutes left to go

It was a gloriously warm August morning, and as I rolled over in bed and stretched, I stopped breathing for a nanosecond when I remembered it was August 17th. I was getting married today!

In line with tradition, my husband had to stay at his brother's house the night before. To give me space and time, he took our five-year-old son Lewis with him. I wasn't happy about Lewis not being with me, but I agreed that not having to worry about him today would be a good thing. I stretched again, thinking this was going to be the last time I enjoyed the freedom of sleeping alone. Looking around my bedroom, everything was in a mess. My wedding dress was hanging on the back of the bedroom door and the clothes I had taken off the night before were on the chair in the corner of the room. I wasn't sure how I should be feeling this morning, but I was pretty sure the sinking feeling in the pit of my stomach was not down to repressed excitement. I had four hours before I needed to get ready for my wedding and yet, I didn't know if I wanted to go through with it or not!

Why wasn't I feeling ecstatic or even happy about finally arriving at my wedding day? The day I never thought I would experience because I was too headstrong. An accusation made by women in my circle of friends and men I had dated in the past. But, more importantly, I never really thought I'd get married because I didn't see myself as fitting the profile. I was too tall, built like an amazon and did not consider myself as pretty enough.

Because of the way my friends and the men in my past described me, as well as the way I saw myself, I was convinced this day was only for other women. The day, I was told, every woman plans for and works towards in a relationship to mark the end of the dating journey. As I lay in my bed thinking about how I got to this point and dreading the day ahead, I wanted to tell myself most women go through what I was going through. I had done quite a bit of reading and most of the literature said both men and women experienced doubts or 'cold feet' leading up to the big day and had reservations about locking themselves down with one person.

I looked up at the ceiling. I knew if I told myself that what I was thinking and feeling were the pre-wedding jitters I had read about, I would be lying to myself. And lying to myself was a trait I had tried hard over the years to eradicate from my thinking. I was determined to always be true to myself and what I was really thinking and feeling. Even if trying to present something different to the world, I tried to be honest with myself. With that thought in mind, I was resolute that I needed to dig deep and analyse what was making me feel so uneasy. But before diving into my reflections, I needed to brush my teeth and make a cup of tea.

Getting out of bed, I grabbed my robe and being mindful that my bridesmaids were sleeping in the bedroom next to mine, I quietly opened my bedroom door and made my way to the bathroom. Carrying out my bathroom activities had become so automatic over the years, it was done with very little thought. This morning, however, I was very aware of my actions when I walked into the bathroom and closed the door. I sat on the toilet and stretched over to the sink to pick up my toothbrush. I squeezed an ample amount of toothpaste onto the brush and popped it into my mouth. Before brushing, I used the toilet and flushed it. Standing in front of the sink, I looked at my reflection in the mirror and gave an involuntary gasp. They say – the eyes are the window into the soul – and my eyes looked dull and lifeless; reflecting everything I was feeling. At that moment, if I was in any doubt that I was making a big mistake, it was evident in my eyes, which had never been able to hide how I felt.

When I had finished in the bathroom, I quietly made my way downstairs and into the kitchen where I put the kettle on. As I stood waiting for it to come to the boil, I knew I needed to come to terms with what I had done before I walked down the aisle. With the tea made, I sat quietly thinking about anything and everything other than the event that was going to take place in little more than four hours.

Finishing the tea, I was about to take the mug into the kitchen and then thought better of it. In one last act of defiance, I placed the mug on the side table and walked away. I quietly climbed the stairs, while thinking Travis – the man I was going to marry – was going to be so pissed when he saw that empty mug on the side table! I entered my bedroom, shut the door, took off my robe and got back into bed.

As I got comfortable, the look in my eyes that I had seen in the bathroom mirror popped into my mind and I knew it was time to start at the beginning and unpick the issues I had been suppressing all these years.

I thought back to the day Travis and I met. It was at a New Year's Eve house party I went to with my favourite cousin, Lenny. When we arrived, Lenny went off to get us drinks. As I didn't really know anybody, I stood by the front door swaying to the music, waiting for my cousin to return and not really taking much notice of anyone. The door was constantly opening and closing as people were arriving in time for the clock to strike midnight and bring in the New Year.

I was about to light a cigarette when I was aware somebody was standing in front of me. I looked up and there he was. Tall, good-looking, immaculately dressed, with an air of confidence and he was looking directly at me. I remember thinking he had the loveliest eyes I had ever seen. His pupils were light brown and he had long eyelashes that curled at the ends. Sensing a slight movement to his left, I noticed the woman standing next to him. She was tall, slim, well-groomed with not a hair out of place and the look on her face was screaming; 'He is mine, hands off!' I remember thinking; ***Wow! She is gorgeous***. When I looked from her back to the man she was standing with, he was still staring at me. At first, I thought I was in the way and he wanted me to move.

As I was about to ask him what his problem was, Lenny returned with my drink. He greeted the man with warmth and familiarity. While they were exchanging greetings and giving each other man hugs, the woman glared at me as if she wanted to scratch my eyes out. I wasn't sure what I had done to annoy this woman and feeling more confident now Lenny was back, I ignored her.

After the warm greeting between Lenny and the man who was staring at me, my cousin turned and introduced me.

'Travis, meet my cousin, Melissa.'

We shook hands.

'Hello Melissa, it is very nice to meet you,' Travis said.

When he let go of my hand, which I thought he held on to a little longer than was necessary, I was expecting him to introduce me to the woman he was with. He did not and she did not look surprised or offended. It was as if being overlooked – as though invisible – was a common occurrence. After the introductions, Lenny made our excuses and dragged me off to meet and greet other people he knew. However, I noticed that wherever I stood when I looked up, Travis was there. At first, I thought it was a coincidence. But after a while, his constant presence was hard to ignore.

Sometime later, Lenny had disappeared again and I was standing alone in a corner dancing to the music. Travis left the woman he came with and walked towards me. When he was standing in front of me, he asked if I wanted another drink. I could see the woman he was with in my line of vision and she looked thunderous. My immediate thought was to reject his offer. But as I opened my mouth, I heard myself accept. He asked me what I wanted and he disappeared into the crowd. He was back before I knew it and handed me my brandy.

'I have known your cousin, Lenny for years,' he said. 'Why have we never met before?'

All the time he was talking to me the woman he was with was standing across the room, alone and looking dejected. Instead of answering his question, I asked one of my own.

'Don't you think it's a little rude leaving your girlfriend by herself, while you are standing here talking to me?'

'She is not my girlfriend, she's a friend. It's New Year's Eve and she didn't have anywhere to go tonight. I was invited to this party, so I suggested she came with me.'

'Is that so? Then, why does the look on her face and her body language say something different? If she is just a friend, why is she looking at me as if she could scratch my eyes out?'

'We have been friends for a long time and she gets a bit territorial. Don't let her behaviour bother you. Ignore her, which is what I do most of the time when she gets like that.'

I am not sure I believed him, but I made the decision to let the matter drop. I was meeting lots of new people and enjoying myself. Anyway, when the night was over, I was convinced I would not see Travis again so I made the decision to have a good time.

As we headed towards midnight, Lenny returned with glasses of champagne and Travis excused himself, returning to stand beside the woman he had arrived with. Champagne in hand, the music was stopped and everyone began to countdown.

'Ten! Nine! Eight! Seven! Six! Five! Four! Three! Two! One! Happy New Year!'

Lenny kissed me on the cheek and hugged me.

'Happy New Year Melissa!'

'Happy New Year to you Lenny!'

We laughed and blew party poppers at each other. Looking around the room, everyone was hugging and kissing and the DJ started playing again.

'Can I have this dance, please?' Travis asked me.

'Of course, you can,' I said, looking over his shoulder to see where the woman he had walked in with was.

'Where is she?' I asked.

Travis immediately knew who I was talking about.

'In the other room, talking to somebody she knows.'

Although I was not completely convinced their relationship was just friendship, I was happy she was not standing in a corner staring at us. We danced and talked through three more dances before Travis thanked me and, I suppose, went to find his 'friend.'

'Hmm… It looks as if you have an admirer,' Lenny said, as he walked towards me with another drink. I did not want him to make a big deal of Travis dancing with me, so did not respond to the comment. But silently I mused about why Travis seemed to have singled me out, and wondered what his game was.

My cousin and I were getting ready to leave the party when Travis walked towards us. He looked at Lenny and there seemed be to some kind of silent communication.

'I am just going to say goodbye to a few people, Melissa. I won't be long,' and with that Lenny walked away, leaving me standing with Travis.

I squared my shoulders and looked straight into Travis' eyes.

'What exactly is going on?' I asked.

'Look Melissa,' Travis began. 'I like you and wondered if I could have your phone number. I asked Lenny if he would give it to me but he said I would have to ask you for it.'

My first thought was; *why would he ask Lenny for my phone number as if I did not have a say in whether I wanted to be in contact with him?*

Before I could respond, Travis said quickly, 'If you don't want to give me your number, let me give you mine. I'd really like to hear from you.'

I suppose it was his willingness to accept my hesitance in giving him my number that made me give in and give it to him. So, before I left the party, we exchanged phone numbers and from the very next day we were in constant contact.

Thinking back to how Travis and I met made me smile. What an evening that was! In the early days, when our relationship was fresh and exciting, I used to thank God that Lenny had asked me to that party with him.

Oh well! Thinking about what life was like when Travis and I first met was all well and good, but things had changed between us since then. And thinking about the 'good old days' wasn't getting me any nearer to addressing the issue of why I was not looking forward to getting married. I had to get to the bottom of the problem.

Casting my mind back, I thought about the early days when Travis and I used to spend a lot of time together. He was either at my house or I was staying at his flat. I remember when I was staying with him for a week. Travis had gone out to work and I was lazing around the flat, watching television and taking it easy, waiting for him to return when my mobile phone rang. When I looked at the caller identity. It was Travis.

'Hello Travis,' I said.

'Hi Melissa! What are you doing?' he asked.

'Nothing,' I replied. 'I'm watching television, taking it easy and waiting for you to come home.'

'I missed you so I thought I'd give you a ring,' he said.

'Ah! That's nice of you to say,' I responded. 'I miss you too. Have you been working hard this morning?'

'I always work hard!' Travis replied. 'I had a few house calls to make today, so it's been busy this morning. Oh! I must tell you, a funny thing happened today, I couldn't wait to tell you about it.'

'What happened?' I asked.

'Have I ever mentioned a woman called Julie?'

'No,' I said.

'Julie is someone I used to date casually.'

'Oh yes…how casual, is casual?' I asked.

'Come on Melissa! It was before I met you. Anyway, there is nothing for you to worry about and I'll tell you why. Well, Julie rang me today.'

I said nothing, waiting for the rest of it. A minute ticked by before Travis said anything.

'Don't you want to hear what she said?' he enquired.

'Of course, I do!' I stated, a little stiffly. 'That is why I'm waiting for you to tell me!'

'Oh,' he said, 'because when you didn't say anything, I thought you weren't interested.'

'Are you going to tell me what she said or not?' I responded.

'She asked if I was going to be in the office. I said I was out and about but would be back by 11:30 am. She said she was going to come and see me. At 11:30 am she phoned to let me know she was outside. When I went out to the car park, she was sitting in her car. She unlocked the car and I got in. I turned to her and asked her why she had come to see me. She complained that she hadn't seen me for a while and wanted to know why.'

'What did you tell her?' I asked.

'I told her that I'm with someone and that was why I hadn't been to see her. Guess what she did then, Melissa?'

'What?' I asked.

'She turned to me and, undoing the seatbelt, she opened the coat she was wearing! She had nothing on underneath! When I didn't say anything, she said, "Are you telling me you're going to pass up all of this because you're seeing someone?"'

'What happened next?' I asked.

'I told Julie it's serious between us. She then said, 'whoever she is, it must be serious because it's never stopped you before.' I got out of the car and returned to my office.'

When he had finished, I had to ask him. 'Why did you feel the need to tell me that little tale, Travis?'

'I wanted to let you know there are women out there who don't care if I am with someone. They want me any way they can have me. I wanted to let you know that if you are ever in doubt, I'm with you because I want to be and not because I don't have choices.'

'So, you thought the best way to let me know that I am with somebody that is considered a 'good catch' is by telling me that story?'

'There is no need for you to get jealous! I wanted you to know what happened. Anyway, I've got to go now. I'll be home about 4:30pm. Love you!'

When something happens that I find upsetting, I have never been the kind of person who reacts in the moment. So, when the call ended, I couldn't stop thinking about what Travis had said. And the more I thought about it, the angrier I became. Why would he phone me at midday and tell me that little story? What game was he playing? Was I supposed to consider myself privileged because he was with me and not one of the many other women he could have had? Well, we will soon see about that! I got up, turned the television down and left the lounge. Going into the bedroom, I retrieved my holdall from the closet and started packing my things. When the packing was done, I went into the bathroom and showered. Returning to the bedroom, I did my hair and make-up, dressed carefully and went back to the lounge, turned up the volume on the television and waited.

At 4:35pm Travis walked through the front door of his flat.

'Melissa! I'm home. Where are you?' he called. 'I hope you are wearing something sexy!'

I did not respond and waited for him to enter the lounge. Travis kicked off his shoes and walked into the room, coming to a halt when he saw that I was sitting fully dressed, staring at the television.

'Melissa! Why didn't you answer me when I walked in the door?'

'I was waiting for you to get home,' I said. 'And now, I'm leaving.'

'What do you mean you're leaving? Where are you going?'

'I thought about that phone call earlier and I realised that you're playing some kind of game with me and I'm not having it. I think it would be best if I go home. But before I go, I wanted to give you the opportunity to explain what exactly that was all about today!'

'I told you what happened today and I thought you understood I was telling you that even though women might be throwing themselves at me, you are the one I'm with!'

'Why then,' I shouted, 'did your little story sound as though you were letting me know that I should be grateful that you're with me and not with one of those many women?'

'Look Melissa,' he began, trying to placate me, 'I have said what I am going to and if you don't believe me that is up to you. If you want to leave that's also up to you. I am not going to stop you!'

'Okay!' I replied. 'If you think you have said enough to convince me you are not playing some kind of game, you haven't. I am leaving now! I need time to think and I'd much rather do it alone.'

I walked into the bedroom, picked up my bag with my clothes and personal items and began making my way to the front door. Getting out of the flat and into my car was my primary focus. It was a shock when I suddenly felt my bag being yanked out of my hand.

'Come on Melissa! Don't be silly. I don't want you to leave. Stay and let's work this out!'

'What is there to work out? You had a visit at work today from someone called Julie who you dated casually. I take it, casually dated means you had casual sex with her and she was almost naked in her car. You had a conversation with her and explaining that the reason you hadn't been to see her was because you are seeing someone else. She then practically throws herself at you to remind you of what you're missing. You tell her it is serious between you and the person you are seeing and get out of the car. When you return to your office, you feel the need to ring me and tell me about the visit and you want me to be grateful that you have chosen me rather than this other woman! What else is there to say?'

'I am sorry if I upset you. I thought you would find it amusing. At least, I now know you can get jealous! Go and unpack and I'll order us a pizza.'

I allowed myself to be led back to the bedroom where I unpacked my clothes and placed the empty holdall back in the closet. That evening, Travis was particularly romantic and amorous. He couldn't stop kissing, cuddling and holding my hand. He told me how much he loved me and we planned our future together.

Thinking back to that event, it was then that the mistrust within our relationship began to surface. There have been countless times since then that Travis has said and done things that we have argued about and he has mentioned my jealousy. I never thought about it before, but suddenly it seemed clear to me he had a real fascination with me being jealous of other women in his life.

The fourth of July, which was seven months after we met, popped into my head. I wondered for a minute or two why that date was significant and then I remembered. That was the day Travis told me we were going to get married. Travis and I were spending the weekend together. We had just finished eating when, out of the blue, he took hold of my left hand. I didn't question his action because he often held my hand. What was surprising was when he put his hand in his trouser pocket and produced a gold ring with a solitaire diamond.

It was not in a box.

Slipping the ring on the third finger of my left hand, Travis said, 'This is to let you know you are mine and we are going to get married.'

'That wasn't very romantic.' I said.

'The fact that I want to marry you should be all the romance you need,' was his response.

Thinking back on what should have been a momentous occasion, I could see where it all began to go wrong for me. Travis didn't ask me if I wanted to marry him and then wait for my response. He assumed that because it was something he wanted, I would fall into line. But in truth, why wouldn't he think that? Because even though I was annoyed at the way the proposal was delivered, I didn't argue the point. I didn't take the ring off and tell him to either come to me with a different proposal or fuck off!

During the next few years, I was gradually introduced to Travis' son from a previous relationship. I met friends, members of his extended family and was sucked into the politics and dynamics of his immediate family. We took holidays together, eventually bought a house together, had a child together and argued a lot! During and after each argument, I had the feeling that Travis was trying every trick in the book to control me. Being stubborn, I resisted his control but I also knew I was doing more compromising than was healthy.

The more Travis exhibited his controlling behaviour, the more I began to emotionally retreat. Thinking back on his behaviour, it would be safe to say, he took my emotional retreat as compliance.

'You know we wouldn't argue so much if you didn't think you knew everything and would just let me do the thinking,' he would say whenever he had the opportunity. This was meant to establish where the blame lay for our disagreements and to make it clear they were my fault. It was getting harder and harder to live with him and the days of feeling happy were becoming fewer. There were days when I wanted to be anywhere but at home and I even began to plot an escape route.

Every now and again Travis mentioned the fact that he intended to marry me but he could not see it happening if we continued to have so many disagreements. We had bought a house and had a child together, so in his mind, it was a foregone conclusion I would want to get married. It didn't occur to him that I might not want to and so using marriage as a stick to beat me with was useless. But, to be honest, why wouldn't he think he could use marriage to get his own way? I had done a good job of sleepwalking through the relationship and masking who I was. Travis was of the opinion that it was every woman's dream to get married. Therefore, it must be my greatest desire. I couldn't really blame him for thinking that especially since I did nothing to make him think otherwise.

Having started on the reflective road of truth and honesty this morning – the day of my fast approaching wedding – I was determined to see it through. Looking at my watch, I knew I had the time. I closed my eyes, lay very still and did some deep breathing to move me to a state of openness and clarity. After a minute or two, I was more relaxed and calm. Looking over at the door where my wedding dress was hanging, I used it to focus and began to mentally travel through the mist of time and all the accumulated events to locate the truth about why I was feeling the way I did. While on my journey, there was one word that kept coming up time and again. And that word was *manipulation*.

We had celebrated the incoming year when Travis announced he wanted to get married before his 38th birthday, which would give us two years to plan it. Even now, a few hours before walking down the aisle and saying, 'I do', I remember how at the time I thought, 'Oh God! How am I going to delay this?'

He must have asked me a direct question because I remember being jolted back to the present and when I looked at him, it was obvious he was waiting for an answer. As panic set in, my immediate response was, 'Why do you want to get married?'

Thinking back, for a nanosecond there was a look of dismay on his face, then there was determination. But I was equally determined, so I went on.

'We are alright the way we are. We have a child. We have bought a house together. Why do we need to get married? It really isn't necessary in this day and age.'

He looked at me and said, 'Every time I raise the issue of getting married, you try and avoid the subject. Don't you want to marry me?'

I wanted to say, 'No, I don't! Not to you.'

Instead I said, 'It's not that I don't want to marry you, it's just that I have started my management course, which is really tough going and I want to do well. And with work, home, and going to university, there is so much going on. I really can't think about organising a wedding as well.'

He continued looking at me so intensely, I wanted to squirm under his gaze, but I made myself stand firm and look directly at him. I knew he was trying to make me uncomfortable and wanted to catch me out in my lie. After what seemed like an age, he said, 'Alright, when does your course finish?'

I wanted to sigh with relief, but I dared not in case I lost ground. 'I have two more years to go,' I informed him. His next statement almost made me shudder.

'Okay,' he said. 'I'll give you until the end of your course. That will give us plenty of time to save up for the wedding and for you to complete your studies. But make no mistake Melissa, I will not wait one day longer than is necessary to see you walk down the aisle with me!'

He went on, 'I am a little surprised you didn't want to get married next year and if I am honest, I think you are being selfish.'

My first thought at that statement was **there it is**! I knew he was not going to let it go and here is the pressure. He was expecting a response from me. If I ignored him, he would know without a shadow of doubt that I had played him and got what I wanted.

I needed to look innocent and make it look as though I had not won this round, so I wiped all expression from my face and made the decision to play along.

'Why am I being selfish?' I asked and that was the opening he needed.

'You have always known I intended to marry you,' he said, 'which is more than I intended with any other woman I have been in a relationship with and as I have told you, many other women have tried to get me down the aisle.'

As I was looking at him, still trying to keep any expression off my face except the appropriate ones, like being contrite, all I could think was; *I wonder how long he is going to keep going until he thinks he has made his point and is satisfied that I have been suitably verbally chastised?*

I became aware that he was expecting an answer to something he had said. Oh God, what am I supposed to say? He was expecting me to reassure him and to be honest, I didn't want to!

I was not in the mood to placate him. I was, however, doing my best to head off an argument that, if I wasn't careful, could last for at least three weeks! I settled on my response. 'I know you have always intended to marry me and I'm quite happy to get married. It is just that I want to finish my management course first.' Wrong response!

'If you know, why are you putting off getting married until after you have finished your qualification?' he demanded.

I thought; **Oh shit! *I walked straight into that and didn't even see it coming!*** At that moment, I knew all my effort to head off a three-week argument was futile and we were going to go there whether I wanted to or not.

'When I started my management course, getting married was not something we were talking about. Now that I have started,' I went on, 'I want to do my best and get a good grade and I think doing a full-time job, being a mother and going to university as well as organising a wedding will be too much at the moment!' I thought I put forward my argument very well.

'I notice you did not mention me in the list of things you think are important,' was his response.

I was getting fed up with the discussion. I wanted it to be over. But like fish being baited and hooked, I was being reeled in.

'What do you mean, I didn't mention you?' As the words left my mouth, I knew the veneer had slipped. My calm exterior had gone and I was in battle mode.

On reflection, this of course was what he wanted and I had played right into his hands. Even though I was kicking myself for being drawn in, the damage was done and the argument I was trying to avoid was in full swing.

As I was waiting for Travis to explain his statement, I remember thinking; 'fight or flight', I could either reduce the emotionally charged situation by apologising and walking away, leaving him to believe he had gained some ground, or I could stand and fight.

I chose to stand and fight!

'Well?' I said again when he still hadn't spoken. 'What do you mean by I didn't mention you?'

There was a look of satisfaction on his face when he realised I had made the decision to battle it out.

'It's obvious to me,' he accused. 'That I am not a priority in your life. You mentioned the three things that were a priority and I am nowhere near the top.'

I was fuming. The bastard! Not putting him at the top of my list of priorities was what he was going to use to punish me.

I gave up trying to remain calm and shouted, 'I am doing a full-time job to help keep the roof over our heads, doing the lion's share of looking after our son and the housework, doing a management course so I can earn more money and you want me to put you on my list of priorities? You are not a child! Why do I have to put you on my priority list?'

And then, I threw the 'clincher' at him.

'If you earned more money, I wouldn't have to do so much and I would have more time for you!'

As the words left my mouth, I was in no doubt about two things. The first, was that I truly believed what I had said and was angry with him for not doing more. The second, was that although Travis was giving the appearance of being calm, there was a look on his face that told me I was going to regret my little outburst.

I left my thoughts hanging and pulled myself back to the present because I didn't want to think about what happened next.

CHAPTER TWO

TOMORROW IS ANOTHER DAY

Time: 6:30am; 3 hours 30 minutes left to go

Instead of thinking about what happened next when I accused Travis of not earning enough money, I thought about what would happen if I made the decision not to get married today.

What would my mother, my sisters and my brother, say? What would his family say? If I left, where would my son and I live? Could I afford to remain living in London or would I have to leave? What a mess! Again, I looked at my wedding dress and the memories leading to this day came flooding back to me.

The thought of what happened next, when I accused Travis of not earning enough, still had the ability to chill me.

He had bellowed at me then. 'How dare you!'

Travis had never raised his voice to me in such anger and I almost cowered in fear. It was with sheer determination that I remained firmly rooted to the spot, refusing to back down or apologise. An inner voice was telling me, if I retreated from my position, I would start travelling down a road I didn't want to be on.

'I dare because it's true!' I challenged.

'Be careful, Melissa. Just because you are at university doing your 'fancy' management course, and you earn more than I do, that does not make you better than me. Don't think I haven't seen the change in you lately. I am warning you. I will not allow you to make me feel inferior. I am the man of this house and I will be respected. You should also be mindful of who you step on when you are climbing that ladder you are on because you might meet them on your way back down!'

It was not what Travis said that was chilling, it was the way he said it. There was such venom in his voice. Anyone listening to our exchange would not have believed he was supposed to love me!

I was stunned into silence.

'I am going out!' he said, 'and while I am gone I suggest you think about what I have said.'

Ten minutes later, Travis had left the house slamming the front door behind him. The minute Travis left the house, my son came out of his bedroom.

'Mum? Is everything alright between you and dad?' he asked.

'Yes darling! Your dad and I had a bit of a disagreement.'

'He sounded really angry,' he said.

'You know your dad's bark is worse than his bite. We had a disagreement that's all. Everything will be fine son. Don't worry. Do you want me to read to you?'

I led my son back to his room and asked him to choose the book he wanted me to read. The story he chose was one we had read before but I didn't question it. I tucked him up in bed and lay down next to him. As I read the book, he asked me questions about the story and we spent the next hour reading and laughing at the antics of the main character. When I had finished the book, my son was drifting off to sleep. I kissed him and switched off the light.

I was about to leave his bedroom when very quietly he said, 'Mum. Are you sure everything is going to be alright between you and dad?' I walked back towards his bed and kneeling on the floor, I wrapped him in my arms and gave him a tight hug. 'I never ever want you to worry about the arguments your dad and I have,' I said. 'Sometimes we can both be stubborn but I want you to remember that we both love you. So, I want you to get some sleep and I will see you in the morning.'

'Okay!' he said. 'I love you mummy.'

'I love you too,' I replied. 'Now, go to sleep.'

I left his bedroom, feeling very disturbed about the impact our behaviour was having on my son. In deep thought, I descended the stairs, went into the kitchen and considered pouring myself a glass of brandy. Needing a clear head, I made myself a cup of tea instead and went into the lounge. I made the decision to wait for Travis to get home. We were going to have this out. It was one thing when we were arguing and bickering, but it's another when our behaviour was causing Lewis to have concerns.

At 10pm, I heard Travis put the key in the door. When he walked into the house, he popped his head around the lounge door and it was obvious he was surprised to see me still up.

'What are you still doing awake?' he said, by way of a greeting, 'Aren't you at work tomorrow?'

'Travis, please sit down, we need to talk,' I said.

He looked uncertain and, for a second, I thought he was going to refuse. But then he looked as though he had come to a decision. I waited for him to take off his shoes, walk fully into the room, choose where he was going to sit because I was sitting in 'his spot' and get comfortable before I began.

'First, I want to apologise for what I said about you not earning enough money. It was unfair and I said it to hurt you. But lately, I feel as though you have been blaming me for something, but you haven't come out and said what the problem is. You're angry most of the time and you never have a good thing to say. We rarely laugh anymore and it's getting really tough to be positive and upbeat for the sake of our son when I feel as though you were trying to find any reason to verbally attack me.'

I stopped talking at that point, waiting for him to agree, disagree or even ignore what I had said. After a couple of minutes, when he did not respond, I continued.

'The concern I have is the impact we are having on Lewis. After you left the house today, he came out of his bedroom very scared because of all the shouting. And you know what? I made the decision that I'm not going to put him through that.

I'm not going to make Lewis live in a household where he's wondering if his parents are going to be laughing and happy or arguing and unhappy. So, I have reached a decision. If we can't work this out and do better together, then I think we're going to have to go our separate ways!'

At this point I had Travis' undivided attention. From the look on his face, it was clear the last thing he expected me to say was that we should split up.

'We have an argument and instead of talking it through and working it out, your conclusion is that we split up!' he said.

'The argument we had today was particularly vicious and if we were being honest with each other, had been brewing for a while,' I said. 'We don't enjoy being together anymore and, most importantly, our behaviour is impacting our son. This is no way to live and I'm certainly not having Lewis grow up in an environment where his parents are constantly arguing!'

I waited for Travis to respond, while thinking, this could go either way. He was either going to agree that our relationship wasn't working and it was time we went in separate directions or he was going to explain his behaviour and do something different. As I waited for Travis to digest what I had said, I couldn't say with all honesty how I would feel if he said he wanted us to stay together and work out our differences.

'Look, Melissa! I know we have had our ups and downs lately, but that doesn't mean we just split up. All relationships go through difficult patches and this is one of ours.'

I looked directly at him and, for a second, I was disappointed that he didn't come out and say he wanted to split because I couldn't see how things were going to improve. Yet, at the same time, while I sat looking at Travis, I told myself I owed it to Lewis to grow up in a two-parent household. This would mean if Travis wanted us to stay together I would have to swallow it. After a couple of minutes when I hadn't said anything, Travis continued.

'I am sorry, I shouted at you earlier and I certainly didn't mean to upset Lewis. It is just that you have no idea how I felt when you told me you had to work extra hard because I didn't earn enough. I know you just said you only said it to hurt me, but it didn't take away the fact that you do earn more than me and when you said that, it made me feel like less than a man. You have achieved so much in the last few years. And although I am proud of you, there are times when I feel as though you are leaving me behind. But that doesn't mean I want us to split up!'

'Okay then!' I said, 'We are going to stay together and you are still committed to this relationship. But I must tell you, I am not prepared to jeopardise the emotional well-being of Lewis so if we are going to do this, your attitude and behaviour have got to change. You seem to forget that when we came together originally, we had dreams about where we wanted to live, the type of cars we wanted to drive. We wanted to have nice holidays and live in a nice house. All that will cost money and the whole point of me doing this management course is to give me extra skills, so I can earn more money!'

'You are right,' he said, 'we did want all those things and I shouldn't feel as though I am being left behind, but I do!'

'Then do something about it,' I said. 'You don't like the job you are doing so, go and retrain to do something you really want to do!'

For the first time in weeks, if not months, Travis had a genuine smile on his face. 'You know, I never thought about going back to college to retrain; that is a really good idea. I will start looking tomorrow.'

I had no doubt that Travis would begin researching to find a college course to sign onto because that would be his way of competing with me. And if that's what it was going to take for him to feel more of a man, then I was quite happy.

Following the heart to heart conversation, we went to bed and as was usual after an argument, we engaged in make-up sex. Afterwards, I lay listening to Travis' deep breathing that let me know he was asleep and I wondered if I had done the right thing by agreeing to remain in this relationship.

Now – on my wedding day – resurfacing from the depths of my memories, I remembered that our relationship improved after we had cleared the air. We got on better together; discussed more and most importantly we stopped arguing. Well! We stopped arguing in front of our son! Life moved on, but I now had to admit that even though we had an emotional clear out after that huge argument, something had changed between us. On the surface, our relationship looked to be in the best of health, but I couldn't shake the feeling that there was something else going on… I couldn't quite put my finger on.

Another memory came to my mind as I lay in bed, savouring the peaceful time alone. I had wanted to move house for a while but knew Travis would not take kindly to the idea because he hated upheaval and disruption. My determination increased however, following an incident at our local church.

'Eleven people were injured in a sword attack at a church in South London.' It was November 28th, and I was watching the television to catch up on the local news. *'The man indiscriminately attacked parishioners – injuring four of them critically – before he was overpowered by members of the congregation. Police have said they are holding a 26-year-old local man in custody.'*

I was not usually prone to flights of fancy and irrational fear but for some reason, hearing the news that there was a 'crazy' person wielding a machete, attacking people in the local church, scared me. Whether Travis could cope with the upheaval or not, I was determined to have the discussion about moving.

After suggesting that Travis went back to college to retrain, it didn't take him long to identify the college course he wanted to sign up to. He was still working full time and had managed to negotiate with his manager to get time off to attend college one day per week. Today was one of his college days and I was upstairs when I heard Travis open the front door. I was about to go down to meet him and inform him about the attack at the church when I heard him talking to somebody. My first thought was that he had brought one of his friend's home with him and it meant I was going to have to wait before I could raise the issue of the attack at the church.

When I got to the top of the stairs, Travis was standing in the hallway and he wasn't with one of his friends, he was with a woman. A young, very attractive woman! They were talking quietly and there was something about the way they were standing together that made me pause. As I was about to walk down the stairs, Travis looked up. The look on his face wasn't one of guilt, but there was definitely something I couldn't quite read.

'Melissa! There you are,' he said in a tone that sounded as though it was a little forced. 'I want you to meet Sharon. We are doing the same college course and I wanted you two to meet.'

'Hello, Sharon,' I said. 'Nice to meet you.'

As I descended the stairs, I was evaluating Sharon and I could see she was doing the same to me. Travis stood in the hallway watching the interaction between us.

'What have you two been up to?' I said in a light tone.

'We have just finished a class,' Sharon responded, looking at Travis. 'And because we've still got some homework to do, Travis suggested we do it here and I could meet you at the same time.'

Even though I suspected there was a deeper reason why Travis had suggested Sharon met me, I didn't have anything to go on, so I parked my suspicion temporarily and instead asked if they would both like a drink.

'That would be great, Melissa,' said Travis. 'As you have offered, I'll have a coffee.'

I turned to Sharon. 'I don't want to put you to any trouble,' she said.

Even though I was being cordial, it was obvious that Sharon was uncomfortable and I wasn't sure if it was something about my behaviour. It could have been the fact that Travis was still standing in the hallway making no move towards the lounge or the kitchen. Whatever was making her uncomfortable, I made the decision to emotionally embrace her. Not only because I wanted her to relax in my home, but also to see what Travis would do. I was in no doubt there was something going on and I was determined to find out what it was.

'It's no trouble Sharon,' I said. 'Besides, I did offer.'

'Well, if you don't mind, I would also like a coffee.'

'Travis!' I said. 'Why are you still standing in the hallway? Take Sharon through to the lounge and I'll go and get the coffee!'

Travis looked at me and again I could not read the look on his face, but there was definitely something not right. I walked past them on my way to the kitchen to make the coffee. As I lined up three cups, got the instant coffee out of the cupboard and pulled the milk out the fridge, my thoughts were in overdrive. Who is Sharon? Why did Travis bring her here? What's going on? Throughout our relationship, Travis had introduced me to many of his female friends and I had never thought there was something going on. Maybe that was stupid of me but I was picking up a vibe between Travis and Sharon.

As I was pouring the water into the coffee of each mug, I wondered if he was having an affair with her. I immediately dismissed the thought, thinking if they were having an affair, why would he bring her here? Most men who have affairs keep their 'bits on the side' away from the family home. So, that couldn't be it! I put their two coffee cups and a bowl of sugar on a tray and prepared to take it into the lounge. Before picking up the tray, I paused and tried to pull the threads of my thinking together.

Travis bought Sharon here for a reason and I needed to find out what that reason was. I was not going to push it, but I was convinced he was playing a game with me. And Sharon was caught in the middle and she had no clue she was in his game. 'Okay! Melissa,' I said to myself, 'let's watch this play out!'

I picked up the tray and made my way back to the lounge. As I walked in, Travis and Sharon were laughing about something that had happened in their class earlier in the day. I placed the tray on the coffee table and handed Travis his coffee. I also noticed the seating position. Travis was sitting on the three-seater sofa and Sharon was sitting on the two-seater sofa. I offered Sharon the other coffee, telling her I wasn't sure if she took sugar and she could help herself from the sugar bowl I had placed on the tray.

'Thank you,' she said. 'I don't take sugar.'

When they had their drinks, I went back into the kitchen to get my tea that I had made while I was making the coffee, but I had left on the counter instead of putting it on the tray. I knew there was a reason I did that, but I didn't have time to evaluate it now, although I knew I would pick up the thought later. When I walked back into the lounge, I chose to leave Travis on the three-seater and sat next to Sharon. My action had an immediate effect. It was as if the air moved in the room because both of them were surprised that I didn't automatically choose to sit next to Travis, which I suppose, was the natural thing to do; as if I was staking the claim to my man!

'So, Sharon!' I said. 'Tell me about yourself. Are you working?'

'Yes,' she said. 'I work full time as a secretary.'

'What made you decide to do the environmental studies course that Travis is doing?' I probed.

'I am a secretary in a company that delivers environmental services and although I enjoy my job, it doesn't pay a great deal. I decided to do the college course to earn more money.'

'It must be hard working full time and doing this course?' I said. 'I know, Travis sometimes has difficulty fitting it all in. Do you have a partner? Children?'

'No!' She said, 'I don't have a partner nor children.'

'There is no need to make it sound like it is the end of the world because you don't have a partner or children,' I said. 'I think you are doing the right thing, getting your career on track first. There will be plenty of time for the rest, later.'

'Come on, Melissa! Enough of the twenty questions!' Travis said. 'Sharon and I have got an assignment to complete that is due in by the end of the week!'

'Okay, then,' I said. 'I will leave you to it. Have you finished your coffee? If so, I will take the empty cups back into the kitchen.'

Travis and Sharon indicated they had finished. I collected the coffee cups and put them back on the tray. I turned to Sharon, smiled and said. 'Don't let him work you too hard!'

I picked up the tray and left the room closing the door behind me. As I returned to the kitchen, I was even more convinced there was something going on. I washed up the coffee cups and thought about my own university assignment that I had to complete. Leaving the kitchen, I walked past the lounge where I could hear Travis and Sharon talking quietly. As I climbed the stairs still thinking about Travis and Sharon, I realised that I had left my tea in the kitchen when I had taken the coffee to them because I wanted to give them time. But I was not sure what I was giving them time to do!

Before going into my bedroom and opening the textbooks to complete my course assignment, I checked in on Lewis. He was sound asleep. By the time I walked into my bedroom, I had made the decision to put all Travis' game playing behind me. I had work to do and I wasn't going to get it done worrying about him.

I opened my textbooks and started reading and making notes and, within a short period of time, I was in student mode and absorbed in understanding the subject matter of my assignment.

About 90 minutes later, I heard Travis calling me from downstairs. I marked all the pages of my books and went to the top of the stairs and sat down on the top step.

'Sh...! You'll wake Lewis!' I said. 'What's up?'

'Sharon is going now,' he said, 'and wanted to say goodbye to you.'

'Goodbye Sharon!' I said. 'It was nice to meet you and as you and Travis will be study buddies, I expect to see a lot more of you!'

'Thank you for the coffee, Melissa,' Sharon said. 'I hope to see you soon!'

Travis looked at me and guided Sharon towards the front door. As they were saying their goodbyes, I got up from the top step and returned to my bedroom. Opening my textbooks, I tried to concentrate, but instead, I heard Travis shut and lock the front door. Although I was still reading and taking notes, only half my mind was on the task. The other half was plotting Travis' movements through the house. He had gone back into the lounge and switched off the television; put everything back in its place; then he went into the kitchen to get a cold drink. I heard him switch off the light and make his way up the stairs and go into the bathroom.

When he entered the bedroom, the first thing he said was, 'Are you going to continue working? Because I'm really tired and I want to go to sleep!'

He was actually telling me to go and find somewhere else to work. I marked all my pages and closed the books and stacked them into a pile. I was about to get out of bed when he said, 'What do you think of Sharon?'

I realised that getting me to close my books was Travis' intent, but not so I would leave the room, he wanted to talk!

'Well?' he prompted. 'What did you think of her?'

'I liked her,' was my response. 'She seemed like a nice woman.'

'She is and we get on really well! She helps me with the writing of the assignments and I help her with the technical side and it works really well!'

'That's great!' I said. 'It's good to have someone to bounce off when you're doing your assignments. I know, because my university study group has been a real asset when getting the work done.'

'One of the reasons I wanted you to meet her,' Travis said, 'was because we have been talking about going into business together!'

'You and Sharon?' I said, surprised, and wondered if that was the hidden 'something' I was picking up between them.

'Yes!' he said.

'Okay! Doing what?' I asked.

'Sharon understands the administration system that would be needed to deliver environmental services and I have the technical skill and contacts. I was thinking we could set up a business and I wanted you to meet her first – to make sure you were alright with it – before I went ahead.'

'You wanted to make sure I was alright with what? You setting up a business? Or you setting up a business with Sharon? Who, by the way, is a very good looking woman!'

'Are you jealous, Melissa?' Travis responded.

'There you go again!' I said. 'What is it with you, always going on about me being jealous about the women you know? Do I have a reason to be jealous?'

'No! Of course, not!' he replied. 'But she does like me and if I was that way inclined, I know it wouldn't take much, but I keep telling you, you're the only one for me!'

I made the decision not to respond to that little statement about 'if he was that way inclined.' Instead, I stored that piece of information away for later with a view to thinking about why he felt the need to say that.

'I think if you feel you and Sharon can work together, you should set up a business. It sounds like a really good idea,' I urged.

Travis was really excited especially because now he had my undivided attention. This, of course, had been his intention when he entered the bedroom and asked me if I was going to continue working. We spent the next couple of hours talking about the development of his business until we had exhausted every possible twist and turn. Due to his level of excitement, it was inevitable he would want to have sex. And as was usual, after having sex, Travis went straight to sleep. Listening to his deep breathing, I replayed the earlier memory of being introduced to Sharon and the conversation with Travis that followed.

He had done a good job of trying to pull me into the excitement of his intention to set up a business and selling environmental services with Sharon. But there was something that didn't feel right. No matter which way I looked at it, I kept getting the feeling that Travis was flaunting Sharon in front of me. The thought made no sense. If he was having an affair with her why did he want me to know about it? But I couldn't shake the notion. The last thought I had before going to sleep was; ***Whatever he was up to – there is nothing I could do about it tonight – so, get some sleep. Tomorrow was another day.***

Chapter Three

Putting Temptation in Harm's Way

Time: 6:50am; 3 hours 10 minutes left to go

'We need to move!' I said to Travis when he had come in from work one day, a week later, and was sitting at the dining table while I was dishing out his dinner.

'We have only just got this house the way we want it.' Travis stated. 'Why the sudden urge to move?'

Since the day of the attack at the church last week, I had been following the investigation on the national news and in the local newspaper. Each time there was an update, the situation seemed to get worse. I wasn't a regular churchgoer so my concern wasn't that I would be attacked while sitting in my local church. My concern was the health and welfare of my son. He attended the nursery not far from where we lived and sometimes the staff took the children to the local park. If there were crazy people walking around he could be harmed if he happened to be in the wrong place at the wrong time.

'Haven't you heard about what happened at the church up the road?' I said, in a tone of voice that was louder than I intended.

'If you want me to listen to your concern, you had better calm down and lower your voice because you know I will switch off if you don't!' Travis said in a tone of voice I was not meant to argue with.

I was livid! Travis knew I didn't scare easily and that I was trying to tell him something important. Yet, all he could think about was using this opportunity to make me sound like I was being unnecessarily hysterical. At his response, I stopped talking. I had finished dishing out his dinner and placed the plate of food on the dining table in front of him. I put the kettle on and was about to leave the kitchen when Travis said. 'What happened at the church up the road?'

Still smarting from his put down, I decided I didn't want to have the conversation and dismissed it.

'You know what!' I said. 'It's not important. Forget I said anything.'

'Why do you always do that?' he said. 'It's as though I can't tell you to do anything. Your voice was getting too loud and I asked you to tone it down. Why is that such a problem?'

'What do you want to drink?' I responded.

'If you don't want to tell me, that's up to you,' he replied. 'I'll have a glass of strawberry flavoured water, if you don't mind.'

I poured the water into a glass and placed it on the dining table in front of him. Without another word, I left the kitchen and sat in the lounge watching the local news to see if there was an update about the church incident. When he had finished eating, Travis followed me into the lounge. He sat in his favourite spot as the item about the churchgoers being attacked by a man wielding a machete was being discussed on the television.

'Is this what you are trying to tell me about when I came in?' he asked.

'Yes! But I was talking too loudly!' I responded.

'That's a bit concerning isn't it? Especially when you consider it is just up the road,' he said when the news item had concluded.

I remained silent.

'When I got home,' Travis began, 'you couldn't wait to tell me about the incident and now that I'm interested, you don't want to talk!'

'That's just it, Travis,' I smarted. 'When I was trying to tell you about what happened in the church, instead of listening to what I was saying, you were more concerned that I was speaking too loudly, insisting I lowered my voice and speak to you in a more sedate tone. Now you've heard what has happened, you are interested and you want to talk about it. Well, I have decided I don't want to talk about it in your time!'

'God! You can be so frigging difficult at times and you wonder why we are always arguing. I only asked you a bloody question!' he scolded.

I did not respond. Instead, I got up and left the room, went into the hallway to retrieve the bag with my university textbooks and returned to the lounge to begin work on my assignment. My intention was to ignore Travis, bury my head in my books and do my work.

Every now and then, I saw Travis giving me a sideways glance. I knew he wanted to talk about something but because I was ignoring him, he didn't know how to approach it. I let him sweat it out. It took about fifteen minutes before he made the decision to voice what he was thinking and for me to find out what was on his mind.

'Where is Lewis?' he said.

I finished reading the sentence I had started before slowly looking up at him. 'He's playing next door,' I said.

'I really want to talk about the incident at the church,' Travis began. 'I can see now why you were so concerned, especially as we have a small child. What do you think we should do?'

'I told you what I think we should do when you came through the front door,' I said. 'We need to move! In fact, I wanted to have this conversation with you last week, when you came home with Sharon and then with everything else that was going on, it slipped my mind!'

Although I expected Travis to pick up on my little dig about Sharon, he chose to ignore it.

'The area is getting worse,' he went on, 'and I think we should move as well, but I don't think we can afford to right now. I have some credit card bills to pay off and an overdraft I am trying to reduce so until I get those things sorted out, though I think it's the right thing to do, I don't think it's possible for us to move right now.'

I expected Travis to resist the proposal I had made about moving because he hated upheaval so I was not prepared for him to agree with me. What I was also not prepared for was for him to state the reason moving was out of the question was because of *his* debt. But I should have known money was going to be a problem.

From the minute we started living together, I had never really become involved in his personal finances. I was aware he had a life before meeting me and that he had a bank overdraft and credit cards, but I never inquired about how much he owed. He tried to get involved in my finances – a couple of times – asking questions like, how much money I had left in my bank at a certain time of the month and borrowing money to buy petrol. But when I realised how he liked to spend, I blocked him. I stopped telling what was in my account and giving him money when he ran out especially because I never asked him for money.

When I stopped lending him money, I began to realise he would book activities without telling me and then expect me to pay for it. This had stopped when, on one occasion, Travis agreed with a couple of our friends that we would attend a concert. He didn't tell me about it until three days before the event. I was annoyed he didn't give me much time to organise childcare for Lewis but agreed it should be a fun evening. It was when I had agreed to go that he let me know I would have to pay for the tickets because he was short of cash. I knew how much money I had in my account to get me through the month and that did not include an expensive night out. When I refused, he was furious, telling me he had already agreed with our friends. When I suggested he tell them we can't make it, he did it under duress and then we didn't speak for two weeks!

We managed the household by agreeing what we both needed to contribute from our individual salaries for the mortgage, household bills, childminding, food, clothes and extras such as outings and holidays. On one occasion, when Travis asked me for money and I had refused, he said we were in a partnership and should share everything. I suggested the partnership went two ways and if he wanted to know what was in my bank account, I should know what was in his. Excluding his contribution to the running of the household, I wanted to know what his personal outgoings were. He became defensive and when I wouldn't let it go, he got angry and what started as a discussion, ended in another huge argument. I had achieved the desired effect. He never again tried to get involved in my finances or ask me what I was earning, though I suspect he was checking my payslips. But from that day onwards, I never asked him about his finances, what he spent his money on, or what his personal debt levels were. So long as he was contributing to his share of the household bills, I left it at that.

'How long do you think it's going to take to clear your debts?' I asked.

'What kind of question is that?' Travis asked. 'I don't know! And before you start judging me remember, I racked up the credit card bills and bank overdraft from caring for this family. So, I can't give you a date. They will be cleared when they're cleared!'

I knew he would blame his inability to manage his money on what he thought was looking after the family; expensive holidays; designer clothes; and lots of meals out! But in reality, Travis liked to spend and refused to deny himself. If he wanted something, he found a way to have it even if he couldn't afford it.

Whenever the issue of money was raised because there was the possibility of an argument, I tended to back off and Travis had got used to not having to address his spending in any real depth. Today, I didn't feel like placating him or feeding his need to live in a fantasy world. I wanted the truth.

'The reason you have credit card debt and a bank overdraft,' I said, 'is because you like to spend and it has nothing to do with you looking after this family!'

The look on his face told me we were going to get into an argument and, to be honest, I was in the mood to fight it out. So, after dropping the bombshell, I waited for the explosion. But it never came.

'Okay! Maybe I'm not as good with money as you are,' he said, 'but having nice holidays or going to nice restaurants and buying nice things for the house is my way of looking after the family!'

'That's all well and good, Travis,' I said. 'But what is the point when the result is that you have huge debts, you are not spending within your means and because you are overspending, we cannot now move, even though we want to!'

During this exchange, in the back of my mind, I was thinking about why Travis was being so cordial. This was not like him! In the past, when I had raised the issue of his spending, Travis had always been very defensive and refused to talk about it. The fact that he was admitting to and willing to talk about his inability to manage his income was an interesting turn of events and I couldn't help wondering what was behind this latest game of his.

'I know you're concerned,' he said. 'But I don't want you to worry about my debts. I'm going to focus on clearing them, but that will take me a couple of years.'

'A couple of years! How much do you owe?' I exclaimed.

'What I owe is not important,' he said. 'Just know that I am going to pay it off. Besides, why worry now? I didn't notice you worrying when you were enjoying the holidays!'

'That's not true and you know it,' I said. 'I'm always concerned about your spending but every time we get into a conversation about your income and your expenditure, we argue.'

'We argue because you are so judgemental,' he said. 'But when we've been on holiday and I buy nice things for the house, I don't hear you complaining then!'

'Expensive holidays and nice things for the house are the things you want to buy,' I retaliated. 'Because those things are important to you. I could quite easily do without them. So, accept that's your thing that's not mine!'

'Hmm....' Travis responded. 'I have told you how long it is going take me to pay off the credit cards and the overdraft so, there's no more to be said.'

'How much do you owe?'

'Don't worry about it. You made it clear it is *my* debt so, it is my responsibility to clear it,' he said. 'Oh, just to let you know, I am going out this evening. Sharon and I are meeting to discuss the setting up of the business I was telling you about before.'

Now I knew why Travis was being so accommodating. He wanted to go out and meet Sharon and he didn't want me to read anything into it or contest his plan. What he didn't realise is by being so cordial he had already raised my suspicion that talking 'business' might not be all he was going to do.

'What time are you going out?' I enquired, 'And why didn't you mention it earlier?'

'I am leaving about 7:30pm and I should be back about 10pm. I was going to mention it earlier and then we got into the conversation about the attack at the church. I have only just had the opportunity to raise it. Is there a problem?'

'There is no problem!' I said. 'Where are you meeting?'

'Err, I think we are going to meet at her place.'

'You don't sound sure!' I challenged. 'And why are you meeting at her place and not here?'

'I thought it would be better to meet at Sharon's rather than here because we could discuss and debate the issues without having to worry about making too much noise, especially after Lewis has gone to bed.'

I was not happy with Travis going to Sharon's home. Even though the explanation given did sound feasible, I think it was the tone of voice he was using that raised my suspicion. It was hard to put my finger on it, but it sounded as though he was trying to convince me that there was nothing going on. But my issue was that if there was nothing going on, why was he trying so hard to convince me? I also reasoned that if he wanted to have sex with Sharon, he didn't have to come up with this lavish plan, he could do that any time.

As I sat silently contemplating, Travis' mobile phone started buzzing. He looked at the screen. 'It is Sharon,' he said.

'Aren't you going to answer it?' I enquired.

Travis answered the phone and although I couldn't hear her side of the conversation, I could gauge what was being said by his answers. I waited until he had ended the call. 'Everything alright?' I asked.

'Yes!' he said. 'She wanted to know what time I was going to get there and what information she should prepare for our meeting.'

'Well!' I said. 'It looks as though she is eager to get started so, you better get ready. You don't want to keep her waiting, do you? And Travis, if you don't want me to think there is something going on between you and Sharon, you need to stop trying to convince me there is nothing going on because by default I will start to believe otherwise.'

An hour later, Travis was dressed and had left the house. I went next door to pick up my son and had a brief conversation with my neighbours. I fed Lewis, read to him and when it was time, tucked him in bed.

I was sitting up in bed reading, when I heard Travis open and close the front door. As usual, I plotted his progress through the house. He took off his shoes in the hallway, went into the kitchen and opened the fridge to get a cold drink. He walked into the lounge, probably checking to make sure I had switched off everything properly and then made his way up the stairs and went into the bathroom.

'You're still up then?' he stated as he entered the bedroom. 'Were you waiting up for me?'

I ignored his question. 'How did it go?' I asked instead.

'It went alright. We got a lot done today. She's really very good at putting things together, like all of the policies we might need and the graphs. We are now in the process of thinking about a name for the company and then we need to get it registered.'

'Good,' I said. 'I am glad you managed to get a lot done.'

As Travis moved around the room carrying out the usual ritual of emptying his pockets and taking off his watch, I was preparing myself for the argument that would follow him wanting to have sex and me saying I was not in the mood. I watched him take off his clothes and get into bed. When he leaned over and kissed me, saying he was tired and was going to sleep, at first, I was surprised and then I was suspicious. Travis never passed up the opportunity to have sex if I was awake when he got home at night. I wasn't one for looking a gift horse in the mouth but I thought I had better enquire after his health.

'Are you alright?' I asked.

'I am fine,' he said. 'I am just tired. Who knew setting up a business would be such hard work!'

'It should be worth it when it is done,' I responded and with that, I switched off the table lamp, got comfortable and before I knew it, I have drifted off to sleep.

For the next few weeks, Travis spent a great deal of time with Sharon setting up the business. There were times when he would get home, grab something to eat, get changed and go out again, not getting back until 10am or 11am at night. Then there were times when he would ring me as he was leaving work and let me know that he was going to meet Sharon and he wouldn't be home until late. Every now and then, Sharon came around to the house, either with Travis or on her own if she was picking up or dropping something off. Each time, I got the impression she wasn't any more comfortable in my presence than she was the first time we met. But instead of evaluating her behaviour, I just filed it away.

One evening, when Travis had left the house, telling me he was meeting Sharon because they had a job they were going to price up. I had just got settled to do some work on my latest university assignment that was due in ten days, when the house phone started ringing. I was in two minds about simply letting it ring and go to the answering machine, but then thought I had better answer it because it could be important.

'Hi Melissa! It's Simone.'

'Hi Simone,' I responded. 'How are you?'

'I'm fine,' she said. 'What are you doing tomorrow lunchtime?'

'Err, it's Saturday tomorrow isn't it? Let me think,' I said. 'I've got to take Lewis to play football in the morning and then he is going to a friend to play for the afternoon. Why, what do you have in mind?'

'Shall we have lunch tomorrow afternoon? We could go to The Lodge, which is always nice!'

'Okay, I look forward to it, we haven't been out to lunch for a long time. Taking account of the things I have to do tomorrow morning, would 1pm be okay?'

'1pm would be fine,' she said. 'I'll see you then.'

Saturday morning was always busy. Travis left the house early saying he had to meet Sharon to go and look at a job and there was a good possibility he would get the contract. While he was gone, the house had to be cleaned. I had taken Lewis to his football training session. When I dropped him off, I went and did the food shopping. When the session was over, I picked Lewis up and returned home. While he was in the bath, I ironed the clothes he was going to wear for the visit to his friend's house. When he was washed and dressed, we went downstairs and into the kitchen where I made him something to eat. While he was eating, I selected the clothes needed to go into the washing machine. Throughout, Lewis and I were laughing about what happened at the football session earlier and talking about what he was going to do at his friend's house for the rest of the afternoon.

At 12:30 pm, I dropped Lewis off at his friend's house and after having a quick chat with the mother of his friend and letting her know what time I would be him picking up, I left to make my way to meet Simone for lunch.

When I arrived at The Lodge, Simone had not arrived. I sat at an empty table and a waitress took my order. When she bought me the glass of wine I had ordered, I sat quietly and sipped it while I waited. Ten minutes later, Simone arrived. She looked around and when she spotted me she made her way towards the table and sat down.

'Hi Melissa,' she said. 'Sorry, I'm late!'

'That's alright,' I said, as I got up and gave her a hug. 'I have only been here about ten minutes. How are you?'

'I am fine,' she said. 'How are you?'

Something in the way she asked me how I was and the way she was looking at me, made me pause before answering.

'I am fine,' I said. 'What's up, why are you looking at me like that?'

'Melissa, I wanted to have lunch with you today because of something my husband told me last night.'

'What did your husband tell you, last night?' I enquired.

'At about 9 pm last night, he went out to the shop because we needed milk and cereal for breakfast in the morning. When he was coming back, he said he was driving down the road and he passed Travis who was coming the opposite way. Because there was a woman in the car, at first, he thought Travis was with you. It wasn't until he drove past that my husband realised it wasn't you. He said whoever Travis was with, the two of them looked really cosy together, laughing and joking in the car! Do you know who the woman was?' she asked.

'At 9 am, it was probably Sharon,' I said.

'Who is Sharon?' Simone asked.

'She is his business partner,' I said.

'His what?' Simone asked.

'His business partner,' I reiterated. 'You know he has been doing this environmental course. Well, he met Sharon on the course and they have decided to set up a business together offering environmental services. Last night they were out, pricing a job they hope to get the contract for.'

'Do you believe him,' Simone asked, 'when he tells you he is out with Sharon late in the evening pricing a job?'

'Why shouldn't I believe him?' I challenged. 'Both are on the same course and Sharon already works in a company that delivers environmental services and Travis has the technical know-how!'

'You're braver than me,' she said, 'because there is no way I would have my husband set up a business with some woman I don't know!'

'That's because you're a very jealous woman and you don't trust anybody. Least of all, your husband, but not everyone is like that,' I stated.

'Hmm... Well! You just be careful,' Simone said. 'These things always start off innocently and then, before you know it, she will be making a play for your man!'

'I have to tell you, Simone,' I uttered quietly. 'If I found out they were having a sexual relationship, even though Sharon would have to take some of the blame, I would put the lion's share of the blame squarely at the feet of Travis because he is the one with the commitment!'

'You really are different,' Simone said. 'There are not many women who think that way. Most would blame the woman. Which is why we don't put temptation in harm's way! So, remember, allowing Travis to run up and down with some woman he has just met at college, could lead to unintended consequences!'

'Thank you for your concern Simone,' I said. 'But I am sure nothing like that is going on. He really is trying to set up a business. I have seen the developing documentation and they are meeting regularly to get it off the ground and I am supporting him.'

'Okay!' She said, 'so long as you know what you're doing!'

For the rest of the lunch date, we talked about my university course, children, work and generally kept the conversation light. But in the back of my mind, I couldn't stop hearing what Simone had said about putting temptation in harm's way!

At 3pm, I told Simone I would have to leave because I needed to pick up Lewis. We split the bill between us and we left the restaurant. When I got to my car, I turned to hug Simone. Before letting me go, she looked directly at me and said, 'Remember what I told you Melissa, just keep an eye out.' With that, we parted and I got into my car. When I picked up Lewis, he was excited and told me about what he had done at his friend's house, but I was only half listening.

Travis was home when we got back. Lewis greeted his father and then went upstairs to his room to play on his Nintendo.

'Did you price up the job?' I asked.

'When we got there,' Travis said, 'the guy told us what he wanted but I don't think he was serious!'

'Why didn't you think he was serious?' I enquired.

'He didn't give me the impression he was prepared to pay for what he wanted us to price up. Anyway, Sharon is going to type up the estimate but I don't hold out much hope,' he said.

'Don't be so pessimistic,' I responded. 'You never know!'

'Sharon is going to be popping around later with the estimate. I am going to check it through to make sure it is all correct and we are going to drop it off tonight.'

'Why can't you pop it in the post?' I asked.

'Because we told him we would drop it off tonight!' Travis challenged. 'Is there a problem?'

'No! There is no problem,' I responded. 'It's just that you have spent so much time with Sharon this week and hardly any time in the house interacting with Lewis.'

'If you want me to stay home, why don't you say so?' he accused.

'I didn't say I wanted you to stay at home,' I countered. 'I was asking why you couldn't put the estimate in the post, rather than drop it off, personally!'

'As you're going to make a big thing of it,' he shot back, 'when Sharon gets here, I will just tell her you don't want me to go out and she can drop the letter off on her own.'

'If you want to tell her that, it is entirely up to you!' I shot back.

'You started this,' he responded. 'All I said was that I was going to drop off the estimate to the customer and you decided to make a big thing of it!'

I could see that we were fast approaching having another full-blown argument and after hearing what Simone had to say, I needed to think.

'You know what Travis,' I said. 'If you need to go out today to hand deliver an estimate that could easily be sent through the mail, you do that. I am going to go spend some time with Lewis!'

I didn't see Travis until 7:30pm, when he popped his head round the door of our son's bedroom where we were playing a board game.

'I'm going now,' he said. 'I'll see you later because after I've dropped off the estimate, I'm going out for a drink with the lads so there is no need to wait up.'

'Bye Dad,' Lewis said.

After a second or two, when Travis realised I was not going to respond, he retreated. Halfway down the stairs, although I could not hear what he was saying, I could hear him on his mobile phone and then he was out the door.

That night after talking and playing with Lewis and tucking him into bed, I watched television and really enjoyed a couple of films I wanted to see. At 10:30pm, Travis still wasn't home so I switched off the television and the table lamp and snuggled down into bed ready to go to sleep. I must have drifted off to sleep because something woke me up. I looked at the clock on my bedside table and it was showing 11:30pm. Travis was still not home, but I heard a car engine running outside the house. The window was open a little and that made the running engine sound louder than it would normally. I didn't think anything of it until I heard Travis' voice. I quietly got out of bed and, without switching the light on so I wouldn't be seen, I looked out the window where I saw a car parked behind Travis' and it looked like Sharon's car. I stood very still, watching to see what was going on. At the same time, I was asking myself why Sharon was parked in front of my house at 11:30pm, when Travis said he was going out for a drink with the lads. This to me, had meant he was going to part ways with Sharon after he dropped off the estimate.

I took in the picture in front of my house. Sharon was sitting in the driving seat of her car and Travis was on the pavement bending down and quietly talking to her through the open window of her car. It was obviously impossible to see either of their faces or hear what was being said, but there was something about their body language that indicated the conversation they were having was intense. After a few minutes of them talking and me watching them, Travis straightened up and I did hear him say, 'I'll talk to you tomorrow!' And with that, she drove off. I quietly scrambled back into bed and tried hard not to breathe too heavily, pretending to be asleep.

I expected Travis to do his usual ritual of checking the house and then come straight to bed but he didn't. After getting a cold drink out of the fridge, he went into the lounge and switched on the television. I must have drifted off to sleep because the next thing I knew, Travis was cuddling up to me and when I looked at the clock it was 3am. It was obvious something had happened between him and Sharon, but instead of addressing this head on, I made the decision to watch and wait.

CHAPTER FOUR

NO FREER,
THAN A CAGED BIRD

Time: 7:10am; 2 hours 50 minutes left to go

I hadn't thought about the *Sharon* episode for a long time. However, it seemed appropriate to think about it now – in my reflective pre-wedding mood – and admit that deep down I had never really addressed the 'Sharon situation'. Instead, I chose to file it in my specially constructed mental compartment, designed to contain issues I don't want to deal with. But I think I always knew one day the memory of that episode would come back to haunt me. However, I didn't think today was going to be the day! But considering the honest self-evaluation journey I was taking, I suppose it made sense to analyse my thoughts and feelings regarding Sharon because I suspected it would help me to move closer to how I got to this point in my life; the actual day of my wedding with Travis!

As I lay in my bed thinking about my life's journey, I was aware of the slight fluttering in the pit of my stomach. This was a feeling I knew well! It was a sign of fear and it could only be linked to revisiting my memories. Even though it was necessary – deep down – I didn't want to analyse how I really felt when Travis and Sharon were spending so much time together. I knew my apprehension was linked to the emotions I had suppressed to cope with the situation. Parking the emotions – at the time – had been key to reducing the fear. But if I was now acknowledging that I was afraid, it meant I was denying my suspicions.

The truth was, I suspected there was something more going on between Travis and Sharon than I was admitting to myself. The night I watched the two of them as Sharon was parked outside my house, confirmed it. There was something about the way they were interacting. And I knew! But I also knew something had changed between them that night. As I climbed back into bed pretending to be asleep, I now know I had also made the decision not to say anything. However, at the time, I had convinced myself I was being clever and was going to play Travis at his own game by not reacting. But in all honesty, I wasn't brave enough to confront it, for fear of the consequences. I would have had to make a decisive choice about staying in the relationship or leaving and I was not ready to make that decision.

The realisation of my weakness was like having a bucket of cold water thrown in my face. I was so convinced nobody would ever want to marry me that I had built a life around my needs and my wants. I was free to come and go as I pleased. No one told me what to do and if anybody tried, I told them where to go! I mistook this way of being, for strength.

From the beginning, my relationship with Travis was testing the perception of myself, but I was completely unaware of it. I compromised on issues to keep the peace; I tolerated behaviour I thought I never would and above all else, I put my head in the sand when I didn't want to face the reality.

Although I had my family and a few close friends, I did not allow anyone to get emotionally close enough to challenge my thinking or tell me what to do. Now, I was being honest with myself, I had to admit that my life and the face I showed the world was not the truth. I had pushed my self-perception that no one would love me enough to want to marry me so far down. Now I had allowed the truth to surface I was having difficulty recognising it. I had unconsciously created and cultivated an alternative reality designed to give the illusion that I was in control of my life. But actually, the lack of control was the reason I had woken up on the day of my wedding, asking myself how I got to this point.

I considered myself footloose and fancy free and hell would freeze over before I allowed anyone to force me to do something I didn't want to, but I was living in a fantasy world, refusing to admit I was no freer than a caged bird. Because I had not given any real consideration to who I was, the fact that I had succumbed to the trappings and expectations of convention was the furthest thing from my thoughts. I grew up in a single parent household and had accepted there was no male parental figure at home. But outside of the family home, I always felt my siblings and I were being judged by wider society. Not having a father was an issue that constantly reared its ugly head; for example, at school when the teacher gave everyone a clean sheet of paper and asked the class to draw a picture of their family. Then, when looking through the gathered-up pictures, the teacher made comments to all the children who had not included our dads in the picture. Although the stigma of living in a single parent household was not as overt now as it had been when I was growing up, the perceived finger pointed by society had left its mark. I didn't want that for my own child. I wanted Lewis to grow up in a two-parent family. When he left the house, I wanted him to hold his head up high and be considered one of the 'lucky ones' because his mother and father were together. Now that I had given my deeply buried thoughts an airing, I could see where I had gone wrong and I had to admit, the position I was now in, was all my fault.

Having completed the cold stark analysis, it was time to travel back to my memories, but before engaging in the deep breathing needed to settle my mind in preparation for my trip down memory lane, I looked at the clock. I had time. I knew this trip back into my memories was going to be difficult because I needed to connect with my emotional state at that time. So, even though I tried to remain calm, I was bracing myself for the emotional onslaught.

Looking at my wedding dress to help me to focus, the last thing I consciously remembered before slipping back into my memories, was the lesson I had already learnt. Lying on my bed on the cusp of getting married, the lesson was; it doesn't pay to lie to yourself; it will always come back and bite you.

Thinking about lessons learnt, took me back to Sharon. The days and weeks following the night she was parked outside my house, I became observant about the way Travis talked about Sharon and the way he interacted with her. Something had definitely changed.

One evening, Travis and I were sitting at home, which was happening more frequently since that night and his mobile phone started buzzing. He looked at the caller identity and before answering, he sneered. The look on his face was such that I thought it was someone he did not want to speak to. I was very surprised when before leaving the room to take the call, I heard him say, 'Hi Sharon, what's up?'

When he came back into the room he still had that look on his face so, I asked him if everything was alright?

'Everything is fine,' he said. 'Sharon is finishing an estimate and wanted to ask me about some of the detail.'

'Is everything all right between you and Sharon?' I asked.

'Why do you ask?' he shot back. 'Everything is fine. She is doing what she needs to for the business and I am doing what I need to do.'

'Good grief!' I retaliated. 'I was only asking because you seem a little uptight!'

'Do you fancy going out for a meal tonight?' Travis asked. 'With your university course and setting up the business, we haven't been out for ages.'

I looked at him wondering what was going on. He had purposely avoided answering my query, opting instead to suggest we go out for a meal.

'Well!' he prompted. 'Do you want to go out for a meal or not?'

'If you're going to be so dogmatic about it!' I shot back, 'I think I will pass. You don't sound like you really want to go out and

I have work to do. Besides, you haven't given me enough notice to find a sitter.'

'Can't you ask Simone or Bella?' he asked. 'We would only be gone a couple of hours. I just think we need some time out.'

This was the first time in a long time that Travis wanted to take me out and I was flattered. I contacted Bella to see if she could look after Lewis for a couple of hours and started to get ready. We managed to get a table at our favourite restaurant, which was only about a 40 minute drive from home. Once the waitress had seated us and bought the two glasses of wine we had ordered, I made the decision to probe. The consequence of my action was probably going to start an argument, but I did it anyway.

'How is the business coming along?' I asked.

'I don't want to talk about the business tonight,' he said. 'I wanted to come out, have a nice meal and not talk about the business or your college course! Okay?'

The tone of voice he used pissed me off immediately because it brooked no argument. I knew something was bothering him and the meal out was a diversion. What I couldn't help thinking was whatever was bothering him had something to do with Sharon.

'If you don't want to talk, that is fine with me,' I responded.

'I didn't say I didn't want to talk,' Travis said. 'I said I didn't want to talk about the business or your college course!'

He was still using that tone of voice. It was the one he used when he was talking to me as if I was an irritant. Suddenly, I'd had enough and asked him right out. 'Why did you suggest going out tonight when it is obvious by your behavior that you would rather be anywhere but here with me?'

'Why are you determined to spoil our meal?' he shot back. 'Good God, Melissa! I thought it would be nice to get out and spend some time together and all you are doing is trying to pick a fight!'

He was right, I was trying to pick a fight, but only because I was angry with him for making me feel vulnerable. At no point did I blame myself or take any responsibility for the way I was feeling. I blamed him. He suggested we went out because he wanted me to help soothe him. And because I was feeling bloody-minded and could see he was feeling out of sorts, I made the decision to kick him while he was down so he could feel some of what I had been feeling. Of course, I did not say any of what I was thinking.

'This all started because I asked a question you didn't want to answer,' I retaliated. 'So, if this meal is ruined, you only have yourself to blame!'

There was very little conversation. Well actually, there was no conversation after my retaliation. Travis and I were sitting on either side of the table, but we could have been sitting on opposite sides of the world. He just stopped talking and I retreated into myself.

Unsurprisingly, the meal out was a flop. After eating our main course, neither Travis nor I wanted or had desert and, by silent agreement, he quickly paid the bill and we left the restaurant. On the way to pick up Lewis, we sat in the car in silence. On the way home, after collecting our son, we sat in silence. When we finally arrived home, I carried my sleeping son upstairs and tucked him into bed. When I had changed out of the clothes

I was wearing and put a robe on, I went downstairs into the kitchen to get a hot drink.

As I was standing waiting for the kettle to boil, Travis walked into the kitchen. 'Why did you spoil our meal out?' he asked.

I could've played the contrite card because I knew what I did but I refused to let it go. 'I didn't spoil our meal out. You did! Your behaviour of late has been dreadful and for the sake of our son I have put up with it, but I don't have to like it!'

He stood for a second looking at me but didn't agree or refute what I had said. He then turned and walked to the fridge to get a cold drink and I turned and waited for the kettle to boil. That night – although we slept in the same bed – I made sure he did not touch me by scooting across to the edge of the bed and even though I got very little sleep, I stayed there all night.

Travis must have woken up really early because when I woke up at 6:30 am, he was not in the bed. I quietly crept out of the bed, making sure I did not step on any of the creaking floorboards and looked out of the window to see if his car was parked in front of the house, or whether he had left for work. His car was not outside the house. He had gone to work without waking me up. Regardless of what was going on between Travis and I, my little boy needed to be cared for. I went downstairs to the kitchen, put the kettle on and prepared breakfast before waking Lewis up to get ready for his day.

When I had dropped him off at the nursery, I made my way to work. I knew I had a pretty heavy day and Travis had to be pushed to the back of my mind.

On the way home from work, I called in at the nursery to pick up Lewis. When I got there, they told me Travis had already picked him up. When I got home I parked the car but before getting out, I sat for a couple of minutes to mentally prepare myself before entering the house. As I walked into the house and closed the front door, my first observation was that I could smell cooking. Lewis was sitting at the table, eating and Travis walked towards me with a big bunch of flowers in his hand.

'I bought these for you,' he said as he handed me the flowers.

'Thank you,' I said. 'What's going on?'

'I heard what you said last night,' he responded. 'I have been difficult to live with recently and I wanted to make it up to you. So, I thought I would buy you a bunch of flowers.'

'Well! Thank you again,' I said, 'they are lovely.'

'After you have changed out of your work clothes,' he went on, 'come and sit down and I will dish up your dinner.'

I put the flowers down on the counter but before leaving the room to change, I greeted Lewis who had been quietly eating, but observing the interaction between us. Kissing him on his forehead, I asked him if he had a good day at nursery and he nodded enthusiastically.

'Do you like the flowers, Mummy?' he asked.

'Yes!' I answered. 'They're lovely.'

'Good!' he said. 'Daddy and I chose them.'

When I had changed, I returned to the kitchen. Lewis had finished eating and was watching television. I sat at the dining table and Travis put a steaming plate of pasta with prawns and mushrooms in front of me. He then went back to the kitchen counter and returned with his own plate and a bottle of wine.

Once the wine had been poured into two glasses, we began to eat. After we had each eaten a couple of mouthfuls and Travis had checked that what he had cooked was okay, he put down his knife and fork. The action was an indication that he was ready to talk. I could have helped him ease into the conversation by looking up and actively engaging with him. But in the time it took for Travis to put his knife and fork down and lean back in his chair, I had made the decision that he was going to get no help from me.

'Melissa, no matter what,' he said, 'you know I love you, right!'

I didn't answer right away for two reasons. One was, I was still feeling bloody-minded and wanted him to know what it felt like to feel uncertain and two, at that moment, I really didn't care whether he loved me or not because I wanted to make him pay!

'Melissa!' Travis prompted, pulling me from my musings. 'You do love me, don't you?'

I knew the delay in answering the question was likely to cause more problems but I couldn't help myself. For what felt like an age but in reality, was probably a split second, I wanted to shout back; *'No, I don't love you, not the way I should!'* And my next thought was what if I was honest and said, *'No, I didn't love you,'* what would the consequence of that statement be? What would I do next? How would Lewis and I manage? Could I upset Lewis' family life to please myself and put my happiness first?'

'Well?' he asked.

I looked him in the eye and said, 'Don't be silly, of course, I love you!'

As I said what I knew he wanted to hear, reflecting on my response, I had to admit that fear of an unknown future stopped me from saying what I really wanted to say.

We continued eating in comfortable silence. When we finished dinner, Travis cleared away the plates and stacked them in the sink, saying he would wash up later.

We entered the lounge together to sit and watch television with Lewis, when Travis' mobile phone began buzzing. He looked at the caller identity and from the expression on his face, a look I was becoming familiar with, it could only have been Sharon. He got up and leaving the room, closed the door without saying a word. Judging from the direction in which his voice was travelling, he had gone into the backroom. Whatever Travis and Sharon were discussing angered him because although I could not hear what was being said, his tone of voice indicated there was a heated exchange.

The phone call lasted approximately ten minutes. When Travis re-entered the lounge, he had a face like thunder. I remained quiet and he was very aware that I was not making any enquiries.

'You know,' he began, 'I don't think this business idea is going to work out with Sharon!'

I looked at him and still said nothing.

'Aren't you interested?' he said.

'I am very interested,' I responded. 'But I also know that when you don't want to answer my questions, there is no point me asking them. I was waiting for you to tell me what is going on!'

As I looked at him, it was obvious he did not like being scrutinized. It was also obvious that he was trying to find the right words to give me the story. To make matters worse, I was in no doubt, that what he was going to tell me was not going to be the complete truth. I waited.

'Sharon has not turned out to be as good as I thought she was and this whole business thing is taking up more time than I thought it would,' he said. 'The business isn't making that much money and the whole thing is giving me a bloody headache! I've tried telling her we are making so little money, it is not worth the effort, but she is determined and wants to keep the business going!'

'The business has only been established for a few months,' I responded. 'As a new business, you have to develop exposure and generate referrals through word of mouth. You haven't been going long enough to establish all that. I agree with Sharon, you should keep it going!'

I knew there was more to this than he was saying and my response was pushing him into giving me more information.

'Look, Melissa,' he said. 'I know you think I should give the business more time and you are probably right. I still think the business idea is a good one but it might be better to do it with somebody else.'

'Why?' I asked. 'When you started the business with Sharon, even though I was not entirely happy about it, you were so excited. What happened?'

'I didn't want to say anything before,' he went on. 'But Sharon has become a little too clingy for my liking and it is having an impact. She wants me involved in everything all the time and that is the reason I am spending so much time away from you and Lewis! I am not prepared to jeopardise what we have for the business. I think I am going to tell her we need to close it down.'

Even though the explanation given sounded plausible, I knew it was a half-truth and I had to determine what elements of the explanation were true and what was a lie.

'I am going out to pick up an invoice from Sharon that I promised to deliver to a customer,' Travis said a couple of hours later. 'Don't worry though, I won't be long.'

As I was putting Lewis to bed, Travis put his head round the door, said goodnight to Lewis and reiterated he would not be long. When he had left the house, I completed the ritual of reading to Lewis and tucking him in. I had an assignment to start but before I began laying out the structure of it, I phoned Simone.

'Hi Simone,' I said when she answered. 'Can you talk?'

'Hi, Melissa!' she responded. 'I've always got time for you! What's happening?'

Simone and I were good friends but so were Travis and her husband Paul. They watched football together and sometimes went out for a drink. Although Travis would never divulge what they discussed, Paul gave Simone snippets of information. And from what she picked up, we knew they talked on a deeper level than Travis had me believe. I was confident I could trust Simone to keep most of what I said between us. But I was not naïve enough to presume she would not share some of what I was telling her with Paul. I didn't particularly care if through the sharing of information Simone provided him with factual information. What I didn't want was for her to share any of my musings. Before starting the conversation, I prefaced it with,

'Simone! I need you to be careful with what to let on to Paul!' She understood immediately.

****

Oh, my God! I returned to the present moment with a start! I had not thought about it before but analysing that thought again now, I had just realised something new about it. *'I didn't mind if Simone relayed factual information to Paul and it got back to Travis, but I did not want any of my musings to be relayed to him!'*

I did not want Travis to know what I was thinking. And that would have been what my musings were; my thoughts. I did not want Travis to know what affected me. I did not want him to know me!

The realisation shocked me out of my subconscious state prematurely and I knew I had to return to pick up the threads of my reflection but I was in fight or flight mode. I knew I had to return to my memories, but the fact that my heart was racing was a clear indication that I did not want to. It took a few minutes but eventually, I had calmed down enough, to pick up where I left off.

****

'Melissa, what is wrong?' Simone responded. 'You know I won't say anything, but you are beginning to scare me!'

'Simone!' I said, 'I think Travis and Sharon were in a sexual relationship and now he wants out, she won't let him go.'

'What!' she exclaimed. 'You must be mistaken. Travis would never do that to you! He loves you too much!'

'I am telling you that relationship is more than just business!' I insisted.

'If you are so sure,' she went on, 'why are you so calm?'

'Who says I am calm!' I said, raising my voice a little. 'I am not calm, I am furious!'

'Well, if you are furious, I would love to see what you would be like if you didn't care.'

'What are you talking about?' I asked.

'I am talking about the fact that you started this conversation by telling me you are almost sure Travis and Sharon were having an affair!' Simone said. 'And you said it so matter of fact. If it was me I would be tearing my hair out and crying. I would want to kill him!'

Simone was right. She would have been tearing her hair out and shouting from the rooftops. I am not going to lie to myself and say I wasn't upset about having to admit there was something going on. But I wasn't upset enough to shout and scream about it.

'Just because I am not shouting and screaming,' I challenged, 'that doesn't mean I am not angry. If I become emotional, I will lose my ability to think clearly. If I had my way, I would pack my bags and leave right now. But I have Lewis to think about and whatever decision I make will affect him. Besides, I still have my college course to complete, which will allow me to earn more money. That's why I prefer to remain calm.'

'Just start at the beginning,' Simone said. 'And tell me why you think Travis is having an affair with Sharon.'

When I had finished recounting what had happened during the last few weeks. I was greeted with silence.

'Oh my God, Melissa, I believe you and I am so sorry.' Simone almost whispered. 'I don't want to say **I told you so**, but I did warn you about putting temptation in harm's way! What are you going to do?'

'Well!' I responded. 'What is interesting is the 180-degree change that Travis has made in the last week. I think I am going to wait and see what happens.'

'Every relationship has its ups and downs,' Simone said, 'and from what you have said, it sounds like Travis has realised his mistake so, I think that is the right decision for now. Besides, if you split up, how would you manage? Promise me, you won't make any rash decisions.'

'I promise, I won't make any rash decisions, okay!' I said, reassuring her.

When I ended the call, I had a renewed vigour in completing my university course.

CHAPTER FIVE

TWO SHAKES OF A CAT'S TAIL

Time: 7:30am; 2 hours 30 minutes left to go

The relationship between Travis and I, although less contentious, didn't exactly settle down and was difficult to describe, following what I, not so fondly had come to refer to, as the '*Sharon episode.*'

He was spending more time at home but I was aware that he did not like me spending time going to university, which was one weekend per month. I was also setting aside a couple of hours most evenings to complete my assignments and meeting with my study group once every two weeks. To show his annoyance, every now and again there would be a little dig about how much time I was spending away from home or studying or on the phone talking to fellow students about the latest assignment. Completing my master's course was very important to me and

I was not going to be deterred. Each time it came up, I placated him or whenever possible ignored the digs.

The business closed and he did not mention Sharon again. It was as if she had never existed. Travis adopted a more considerate and supportive role in the house, helping with the cooking, food shopping and cleaning. He also spent more time with our son, almost appearing to be the doting father. When we attended family gatherings, at some point, at least one of the women turned to their male partner and said; 'Why can't you treat me the way Travis treats Melissa?'

When these comments were being made, I stood there silently and smiled. Because what members of the family and my close circle of friends didn't know was that I had almost completely, emotionally withdrawn from Travis. It was as though I was playing the role of a character and as long as I was 'in role' I managed the facade.

The realisation that I was emotionally withdrawn, did not become fully apparent until the night I phoned Simone and after letting her know my suspicion about Travis and Sharon, she wanted to know why I was so calm.

I didn't think anything of Simone's statement during the weeks that followed, until one day, while driving to work and thinking (which was my usual practice when in the car alone) I realised that I had put my emotions in stasis. I was convinced that if I wanted to continue to have good mental health and be there to protect and care for Lewis, I had to protect myself emotionally until I could find a way to leave Travis and manage financially.

The interesting thing was Travis' behaviour. It was as though the withdrawal was tangible. He cuddled up to me in bed at night and asked if I was alright, even when we'd had a pleasant evening. He began apologising for little things, something he seldom did in the past and, worst of all, he began talking about our wedding more frequently.

Most of the time, I felt as though I was undercover. I had carefully locked away my emotions so Travis could not hurt me, but I still had to look as though I cared when it was appropriate, get annoyed at the required time and smile or laugh when expected, but none of it really touched me. And I became good at managing the dual roles.

Role number one was Melissa: partner to Travis and mother to Lewis; living the dream of going on holiday to exotic places and driving nice cars; keeping my opinions to myself and dumbing down my level of intelligence to prevent him from feeling inferior. While constantly thinking – I am living with a man I would leave in two shakes of a cat's tail – if I had the financial income to manage on my own.

Role number two was Melissa: the freethinker and free spirit; with my own opinions, aspirations and ambitions. Who, away from Travis, was outgoing, courageous and a risk taker, with a clear sense of direction, climbing the career ladder and in the process of completing a management course designed to significantly increase her income and unlock the gate to freedom.

One Friday evening, when I had taken the day off work to concentrate on completing the latest of what seemed like numerous assignments and I had not cooked because we always got takeout, I heard Travis coming through the front door. I called to him asking what he wanted to eat. He walked into the back room where I was working and placed two wedding magazines in front of me.

I looked up at him confused.

'Where did you get these magazines?' I asked, quickly glancing at them because I was trying to finish the paragraph I was working on.

'I bought them today when I went into the newsagent,' he replied.

'Why?' I asked.

'Because I think it is about time we started thinking about our wedding,' he replied, with a hint of a challenge in his tone.

I knew I had to handle this carefully, otherwise it would dissolve into an argument that I really couldn't afford right now because it would take energy I did not want to use.

'Look, Travis,' I placated. 'I know you want to start planning the wedding but look at this table.' I spread my hands out to indicate the number of books and paperwork I was ploughing through. 'Towards the end of the academic year, the course tutors always increase the number of assignments and I am snowed under. Planning the wedding will have to wait.'

'Why do you keep putting it off? Is it because you don't love me?' he stated.

'Don't be silly!' I responded. 'You can see I have a lot to do and I am determined to get through it. You are making me sound unreasonable, but we have already had this conversation and you agreed we could get married when I had completed my management course. Why the sudden rush?'

As he stood there looking down at me, I could see a look on his face that said he was going to get his own way. The problem was, I was equally determined to finish what I started and I was not going to allow him to disrupt or deter me.

'You didn't answer my question,' he said. 'Do you love me?'

'Of course, I do!' I shot back, without hesitating because I wanted this conversation to be over. 'But what has my loving you to do with me finishing this course?'

'Do you want to marry me?' he asked.

'Yes!' I said.

I should have been listening more carefully but because my mind was still on my assignment, I stepped straight into the trap that I was trying to avoid.

'If we are going to get married when you complete your course, we have about a year to organise it,' he said, 'We need to book the venue we want now to make sure we secure it.'

'Okay!' I said, still only half listening. 'I forgot how difficult it can be to get decent wedding venues.'

'Good,' he said. 'Now we have established that will you stop fighting me and being difficult, just do what I tell you because you know I'm a better organiser than you are.'

And that was it! All my effort to not get into a fight was lost with that last sentence and understanding dawned on me about what he had been trying to do.

I slowly stood up and looking directly at him, launched into a tirade of obscenities.

'Who the hell do you think you are, talking to me as if I am a child?'

For a second, he stood rooted to the spot and did not say anything. It was probably because he thought he had won the battle and wasn't expecting my response.

'You manipulating bastard!' I shouted. 'You knew I had the day off to work on my assignment and you counted on me being distracted so I would relent and bow to your will as though I don't have a brain, the will or thoughts of my own. If the life you want to create is to have the little size ten at home who knows her place and defers to you on all things, you have the wrong person.'

With that said, I walked out of the room before he could say anything to defend his actions. We did not speak for the rest of the evening and there began the non-speaking, for two whole weeks! I felt my reaction was justified because I had already made it clear I couldn't realistically get married until I had completed my management course. He was not happy with the answer and I remember we argued because he could not get me to change my mind. But he seemed to accept it.

However, if truth be known that evening after we argued, I sighed a sigh of relief that we were not going to get married any time soon. In fact, I was silently revelling in the fact that I had managed to put off the wedding for a couple of years. It left me with a permanent smile on my face for almost a week!

****

Back in my bed in the present moment, I was straddling a fine line between the conscious and subconscious. I was analysing how I could have been so happy putting off the wedding and yet feeling so unhappy about what most people considered should be the happiest day of my life. Something was very wrong and I needed to be honest with myself about what that something was. I tossed and turned on my bed, knowing that the time was getting nearer for me to get up and start preparing myself for the day ahead. I also knew I had been putting off this moment and it was time to face my fears and stop hiding.

The word *trust* kept popping into my thoughts. I had to acknowledge I didn't trust the man I was going to marry! I didn't trust him on any level. I think I'd always known he was a liar and a manipulator with a leaning towards being downright dishonest. Even when he said he loved me, I never quite believed him. He once told me I was the only person he would ever marry, and I never believed that either. So, the question was, if I did not believe that he loved me and I do not trust anything he says, why was I marrying him? The answer to the question was somehow out of reach, fluttering around on the periphery of my thoughts, but I couldn't quite catch it.

****

After my explosive retaliation, I was prepared for the silent treatment and it didn't bother me as much as it would have done before the 'Sharon episode,' which had taught me to lock my emotions away. In fact, if I was being honest, receiving the silent treatment gave me some breathing space. I didn't have to engage in his nonsense and I could spend quality time with Lewis. My studies were going well because I could concentrate on my management course and best of all, as long as we were not speaking, I could sleep in the spare room and I wouldn't have to have sex!

However, the two-week 'Cold War' ended when I got in from work and Travis asked me what I wanted for takeout. My first thought was; 'Oh shit! This means the end of the 'Cold War' and he is going to want sex tonight.' Even though he was ready to make up and have 'make-up sex', which had never been my thing, I could have made the decision to continue not speaking to make my point. I did however, think it wasn't fair for Lewis to be living with his parents not speaking to each other and instead of a happy home, he was living in the decidedly chilly atmosphere we had created. What I realised however, was that the length of the time the silent treatment went on for was always determined by Travis. If I tried to talk to him before he was ready, he ignored me and by allowing him to get away with that behaviour, I had given him the control to set the terms.

So many choices! I was aware that I had to make the choice about whether I was going to accept the end of the silent treatment. I now realised that I could do something different and didn't have to tolerate Travis' behaviour. However, the difficulty was believing that the choices open to me were real and not simply notional. I made the decision to accept the olive branch knowing that when Travis decided to end the silent treatment, we would return to speaking to each other without discussing the issue that had caused the fallout and without an apology. I knew that I was not going to let this go, but instead of addressing it, I stored it away with all the other issues, which was my way of bolstering my resolve and not letting him touch me emotionally. Unfortunately, the consequence of developing this thicker skin was that being emotionally distant had become a natural way of functioning for me.

'What do you think about having a break and going away for a week?' Travis stated after a couple of days of getting back to normal. 'We could find something cheap and cheerful?'

Inwardly, I groaned. Travis tended to make his statements sound like a question, but they really weren't statements because he had already decided. And this statement was made just as I walked in the door from work. Travis employed this tactic of telling me his plans before I had dropped my handbag and taken off my coat, to ensure I had no time to think and I was usually tired, distracted with other things and would simply agree. We had not long come out of a two-week 'Cold War' and had been getting on so well that I didn't have the heart to say no. I did however, have exams coming up and I wanted to ensure I did well especially on the finance exam, which had never been my strong point. I knew I would be happy with a pass, but I was so weak on finance that even to get a pass I would have to study hard. Besides, if I failed the finance exam I would be unable to go through to the final year.

'Okay,' I said, as I was taking my coat off and thinking about what I was going to do for dinner, 'I have exams coming up, but a holiday seems like a good idea. Where are you thinking of going?'

At that point, I turned and looked directly at him, waiting for an answer and I caught a look of malice on his face before he could shut it down.

Instead of answering the question as to where he wanted to go for the holiday, he asked, 'When are your exams?'

I was trying to think quickly to make sure I didn't commit myself to something that would be a problem because even though I couldn't fully read it, that look on his face told me I had to be very careful. I tried to do a quick calculation to think about how much revision I had to do, when I had to do it and how much time I would need.

'My exams are on April 3rd,' I said.

'Hmm,' was the only response I received; I didn't quite know what to do with that and I carried on.

'You didn't answer me, where are you planning on going?'

I kept using the word **you** because I suspected this was not going to be a conversation. He had already done the thinking and expected me to agree.

He opened his laptop and proceeded to tell me about a one-week all-inclusive holiday in Portugal that he had seen. This confirmed my suspicion that he had already done the research.

'Mum, I'm hungry,' Lewis shouted from his bedroom and he was my first priority. As a result, I was only half listening to the information about the holiday.

'I have to go and sort out dinner,' I said, after another couple minutes of listening, all the while annoyed that he had got in before me and yet I was the one sorting out dinner.

'Before you go, what do you think about the holiday?' Travis asked.

'It sounds great. Let's go for it,' I responded.

'Okay, I'll get it booked and give you the dates,' he said.

I left the room, ran up the stairs to greet Lewis and asked him about his day.

The following day while at work, Travis rang me. 'I have booked the holiday and the resort looks really great,' he said. 'Can you make sure all the passports are up to date? Oh, and by the way, the dates for the holiday are March 22nd – March 29th. See you when you get home.'

When the call ended, I checked my diary for the dates because I had to book annual leave from work. The dates were booked for five weeks away so that was okay. But, it was at that point that I almost had a heart attack. I was so angry I couldn't speak. He had booked the holiday for a week before my exams, cutting into my revision time. I wanted to kill him. And then I thought back to the night before, when he was telling me about the holiday and the vague response he had given me when I told him my exams were on April 3rd. I suspect he had already identified the dates and had no intention of changing them. He also took advantage of my distraction of engaging with Lewis.

Oh God! What was I going to do? There was no way he was going to change the dates and even if he agreed to, there would probably be a charge, which he would use to 'beat me over the head with.' I went through the rest of the day flitting between emotions. One minute I was angry, the next I was frustrated and then disgusted for allowing myself to be railroaded into a position that was going to cause me untold headache and increase my anxiety if I tried to encourage a change of plan.

When I got home after work, I was so hyped up that before I had even taken off my coat and put down my bag, I went straight into the lounge, which is where I knew he would be and waded straight into the issue.

'Why did you book the holiday from March 22nd – March 29th, when you knew my exam was on April 3rd? Why not book the holiday after April 3rd when the exams are over and I could have relaxed?'

'They were the only dates I could get,' he said. Besides, it is before the exam date so what is the problem? God! All you ever do is complain. Nothing I do is good enough for you. You told me to avoid April 3rd, so I did and yet you are still not happy.'

Travis had a way of turning the tables to make our disagreements sound as though it was my fault and, on this occasion, it was no different. When he made the statement about my complaining, it made me sound as though I was being unreasonable. There had been times in the past, when if issues like this had come up and he blamed me for not appreciating his efforts, I would have backed down and tried to reassure him that was not the case. However, my exams were very important to me and I wouldn't let it go.

'So, you avoided April 3rd because that is my exam date and when am I supposed to get the revision done? I know what you are like, nearer the date when you get into the holiday spirit, you are going to be expecting me to run up and down, buying Lewis's holiday clothes, making sure he has entertainment for the trip, and you have already asked me to sort out the passports. By the time I have sorted all that out, it is going to eat into my revision time.'

By the end of my speech, I could feel myself getting more and more irate as I prepared myself for the battle ahead. There must have been something in my demeanour because instead of a full-blown battle, what he said was, 'It will be fine. All you have to do is bring your revision books with you.'

'How is being on holiday and revising supposed to make me feel better?' I said. 'To make matters worse, you know that if Lewis gets ill the both of you will expect me to stop what I am doing to provide the care he will need.'

'You sound like you don't want to go. I have already told Lewis about the holiday, but if you don't want to go, all you have to do is say so and I will cancel it.'

There it was! I could have made the choice to put myself first and concentrate on revising for my exam. But I knew the point of Travis saying he had told our son about the holiday meant that I would have to bear the full responsibility of disappointing him. I was trapped and he knew it. I left the room without saying another word.

For the rest of the evening, I could not shake off the feeling that the reason Travis had booked the holiday when he did was to prevent me from passing the exam. But each time the thought entered my head, I kept shaking it off as nonsense. There was no way he would do such a thing. He had his 'ways' but he could not be that vindictive, surely?

A week before we were due to start our holiday, the activity of making sure the luggage was travel worthy began in earnest. I bought the necessary clothes and made sure all our swimming and beachwear was upgraded, ready for packing.

'Have you bought the swimming goggles?' Travis asked three days before we were due to fly.

'Yes,' I said.

'Have you bought the sunscreen?' he asked thirty minutes later.

'Yes.'

'How many pairs of shorts and T-shirts have you bought for Lewis?' Travis asked. 'I want to make sure he has got enough.'

'I have bought enough,' I responded. 'What's the problem?'

I was trying to study and didn't appreciate being interrupted by a series of questions, but I knew he was leading up to something.

'There is no problem and there is no need for you to use that tone of voice,' he said. 'I wanted to know how many clothes you are bringing because I don't think I am going to have enough room in my suitcase and I noticed your case is only half full.'

'My case is only half full,' I said, 'because I am leaving room for the reading material, I will need to bring with me, so I can revise properly!'

'You can't be serious! Are you really going to be revising while we are on holiday? The whole point of being on holiday is to relax so, how can we do that as a family, when you are revising!'

I could not believe we were going to have this argument three days before we were due to travel. Planning for the holiday, working, managing the home life and there being no mention of revising on holiday had lulled me into a sense of false security. But the minute the statement about my seriousness to revise on holiday was made, the negative thoughts I had been having on and off that Travis wanted me to fail my exam came back full force. I was so shocked, for a minute or two I couldn't say anything.

'I asked you a question,' he said, 'are you seriously going to revise on a family holiday?'

I closed the book I was revising from, turned my chair around to face him and looked him straight in his eyes.

'We have had this conversation before,' I said. 'But if you have forgotten, let me make it clear to you again. When you booked this holiday, I said to you at the time that I would not have enough time to revise and when I got back, I would only have five days before the exams.'

'I also told you that it would mean I would have to revise during the holiday. You are right, it is not ideal, but you knew the situation and the timeline I was working to. You said nothing at the time and it is a bit late to bring it up as an issue now.'

'Who do you think you are talking to?' was his response. 'Don't use that sanctimonious tone or blame me because you are selfish enough to prioritise your study ahead of the needs of your family.'

There was no way I was going to fall into this. I stayed calm.

'Completing this qualification is important to me. And to do that, I need to pass the exam. If the fact that I need to revise means you would prefer I did not go on the holiday, then so be it.'

All this was said while I continued to look him straight in the eye.

He must have seen something in my body language communicating that I meant every word. He sat and looked at me for what seemed like an age, but in real time was about two minutes. At the end of the staring contest, he got up, said he was going out and left the house. He did not return until close to midnight and although I heard him come in, I pretended I was asleep.

The following morning, we were all up early. I went out to do the food shopping, washed the clothes needed for the holiday and finished the packing. Travis packed his own case.

'Where are the passports?' he shouted from the bottom of the stairs.

This was the first time he had spoken directly to me all day following our disagreement the day before. To show my annoyance at his behaviour, I was not going to answer. Thinking I should show more maturity, I thought better of it.

'The passports are in the safe,' I replied without going to the top of the stairs and addressing him directly.

I finished packing and reading to Lewis and when he was settled in bed, I went downstairs to the lounge.

'What is wrong with you?' Travis asked, as I walked into the room. 'You are behaving as though I have done something to piss you off when I should be the one that's pissed off.'

'What are you talking about?' I asked, not understanding where this conversation was going.

'I don't know what has got into you lately,' he said. 'It is as if you are purposely picking fights with me or saying things to annoy me. Why can't you behave normally?'

'What do you mean?' I queried.

'You know what I mean!' he said. 'Ever since you have been doing this damned course of yours, you have changed. Everything else has to take a back seat and your studying and attending college is the priority.'

The first thought that came to mind was 'here we go'. I knew this would come up. I knew it was burning him to have this argument about my university course, but to have it today before we were due to travel was a change in tactic. I silently counted to ten before I answered.

'Why are you saying I have changed?' I challenged. 'Why don't you admit that you didn't think I would get this far in completing the course and that it is your attitude which has changed because you do not want me to complete it.'

I went further before he could respond.

'I have no idea what you are afraid of, but I can tell you your fear is unfounded. When I have completed this course, it will allow me to earn more money, which will be better for our family because we will have more money to spend. I don't understand what your problem is?'

'That is just it,' Travis began. 'Since starting your course, you have become more bossy and argumentative. What happens when you start earning more money as well? I don't think you can see what your determination to complete this course is doing to our relationship.'

At this point, I felt myself beginning to get seriously angry. For a second or two, I didn't know how to respond and said nothing. When I opened my mouth however, I don't think I was sure what was going to come out, but I knew for sure it wasn't what I said.

'How dare you!' I said raising my voice because I knew it would anger him.

'I bet this has been in the back of your mind for a while. I am surprised it took you so long to come out with it. Ever since I started getting decent marks for my assignments, I have felt a change in your attitude. I wasn't sure what had caused it, but now I know you didn't like the fact that I was doing well and you wanted me to fail. It is ridiculous. As my partner, you are supposed to be supporting me the same way I would be supporting you if you were doing this course. But instead you have the gall to sit there and tell me that if I continue with this course, you have concerns about our relationship! You need to get over yourself because I am not going to stop until I have completed it.'

I wish I could've taken a picture of the look on his face. He was furious.

'You have decided to put the completing of your course ahead of our relationship and our family. That is so typical of your selfishness. But let me remind you of something, you can say what you like, using fancy words and fancy phrases you have learned at college, but you need to remember where you are coming from because the higher you climb, the greater the fall! When this family falls apart, I hope the sacrifice you have made for your qualification keeps you warm at night!'

With his statement made, he almost knocked me over as he brushed past me and left the room. He went up the stairs and five minutes later, I heard him run down the stairs again and leave the house, slamming the front door, without saying a word.

I started to laugh. I stood in the same spot for at least five minutes and couldn't stop laughing. When I finally stopped, I realised that I was laughing because by refusing to bend, I had finally pushed Travis to say what had been on his mind for months. As I began to calm down, fight or flight was my primary thought. I remember thinking I needed to leave. I can't stand this anymore! The situation between us was getting worse! How could I marry somebody who didn't respect my academic ability and simply wants to control me? Hot on the heels of the self-imposed questions were equally damning answers. You don't have anywhere to go, yet!

I had been tolerating Travis' bullshit for years so, why should this situation be any different? I needed a better income to ensure I could look after Lewis, who I had no doubt would be living with me and the time was not yet right to do something about it. The situation between us was not getting any worse; it had always been like this. The difference was that I allowed him to feel as though he was in control and of late I had pushed back.

However, the most concerning question in need of an answer was, knowing what I do now. How could I marry someone so determined to limit my achievements? He was keeping me mentally locked in a box to bolster his ego and prevent me from being myself. I recognised that I needed time to answer these questions and, as had been usual during the last few years, I simply shelved them.

Pulling myself together, I filled the sink with hot water to wash the dishes. Immersing my hands in hot soapy water always helped me to focus my thoughts, so I set about vigorously washing up. By the time I had finished, I was much calmer and able to put the whole disturbing conversation behind me. Staring into space and functioning almost like a robot, I rinsed the last dish and placed it on the dish rack to drain and dry. I picked up the dishcloth and was drying my hands when I experienced a feeling of fear so profound, that it felt as though I had been hit in my stomach and left me breathless. Holding onto the sink, I stood for a couple of minutes, waiting for the feeling to wash over me.

I had heard that the brain is a powerful organ and although I kind of knew it, never was I more sure than in the two minutes I stood holding onto the sink.

In the time it took for the feeling of fear that had infiltrated my thinking to disappear, I had analysed the cause. I was able to look inwards and knew what was to come with regards to my future. It was imperative that I finish the course because my relationship with Travis was not going to survive. Without feeling shocked, sad or remorseful, I let go of the sink and knew what I had to do.

Walking through the now quiet house with determination, I went into the study, opened my books, fired up my computer and worked on completing the assignment I had to submit in a week's time.

CHAPTER SIX

The Pressure

Time: 7:50am; 2 hours 10 minutes left to go

I failed the finance exam!

I was so upset. Blaming Travis for booking our holiday when he did was the easiest thing to do to feel better about failing the exam, but it was not until I had a tutorial session with my university tutor, that I accepted the real reason for the failure was my lack of confidence in my ability.

I didn't tell Travis about failing the exam. Not telling him was in part due to the fear of what he would say. I have no doubt he would tell me I had overstretched myself and I didn't want to hear him gloat. But more importantly, I refused to admit to the failure and saying it out loud would have made it more real. I had failed and I knew it was my fault.

When I got the results, I made an appointment to see my tutor. Entering his office, he sat me down, while at the same time shaking his head with a 'Tut! Tut! Tut!' When I asked him why he was shaking his head, he said. 'You were determined to fail the exam and you did!'

I was shocked at his statement. The only thing I had focused on for weeks was getting through the exam because I knew it was my weakest area. And when I told him so, he responded with, 'Exactly! You were so caught up in getting through the exam, you didn't spend enough time thinking about what you *knew* about the subject matter against what you didn't know.'

I tried to defend myself, but eventually had to concede that he was right. Exams had never been my thing and my anxiety about passing the exam was so overwhelming that being afraid of failure was all I could think about. At the end of the conversation with my tutor, I was in no doubt that I had created a self-fulfilling prophesy. As I was leaving his office, my tutor said, 'Give yourself a chance, Melissa. You are quite capable.'

He gave me the date for the re-sits that were scheduled for a month's time and the name of students to contact who were good at providing finance mentoring. I had already failed, so the only direction for me to go was up. Selecting the person I wanted as my mentor, I spent every spare minute either studying the formulas or being coached through them. I was determined to pass the re-sit exam because I was going through to the second year.

One Saturday morning, after I had finished food shopping and was on my way home singing along to music in my car, I realised I was feeling good about myself. The conversation I had with my tutor, just after I had failed the first exam, was at the forefront of my mind. At the time, I was so anxious that I didn't think or really understand what he was saying. That conversation was three weeks before and working with my finance mentor had worked wonders. The anxiety had passed and as I was driving home and reflecting on what he had said, it took on a new meaning. My tutor implied that I had prevented myself from passing the exam the first time. At first, when the idea popped into my thoughts, I dismissed it as ridiculous. Why would I do that to myself? I really wanted to pass the exam. But now I know he didn't mean that. What he meant was my self-doubt and negative thinking – in essence – my fear, had paralysed me into believing I could not pass the exam.

The following Thursday, I booked an annual leave day and re-sat the finance exam. Although I was not expecting a fantastic result, I knew I had done enough to scrape a decent pass. I waited for confirmation that I had passed it. My latest assignment was completed and submitted on time. I knew I had grasped the concept and had produced a good piece of work, so I was expecting a good mark. I was feeling great.

The relationship between Travis and I also appeared to have turned a corner. I am not sure what happened, but it appeared that once Travis had got the issue of my college course interfering with our relationship off his chest, he seemed to be more amenable. Although it felt a little like the calm before the storm, I made a concentrated effort not to evaluate his change in behaviour until it was unavoidable. In part, this was because I was afraid to look too closely because investigating the reason for the change would take up valuable time and I wanted to devote my spare time to completing my course successfully.

Since returning from the holiday, life at home was much calmer and there appeared to be less pressure for me to meet everybody's needs. Travis was more engaged with family life which had taken some of the pressure off. But more importantly, there was no more mention of the wedding.

Although Travis and I had less disagreements, something happened causing me to pause. As was usual for my birthday, Travis organised a barbecue to be held in our garden. In comparison to mine, his family was large and very dispersed. In the early days, when Travis suggested holding the barbecues, it served two purposes. One; was to celebrate my birthday and the other; was that it was a good way of bringing his family together. As a result, not only family but friends were invited and it always ended up being a big affair. The challenge was always catering for large numbers of adults and children and the amount of preparation needed to ensure the event went without a hitch.

At first, finding the time to do all the shopping, prepare all the meats and entertaining the guests for a whole day, was enjoyable even though it was hard work. But as the years passed, I began to dread the barbecues. I no longer saw them as a celebration of my birthday but a day that took a lot of time and energy to prepare for and left me exhausted. And I vowed this year would be the last one.

The house and garden were ready to receive guests and I was getting changed when Travis entered the bedroom.

'Melissa!' There was something in the way he said my name that made me stop what I was doing and look at him.

'What's up?' I asked.

'It is your birthday, so I don't want you to get upset,' he said.

'That statement sounds like even though you don't want me to be upset,' I responded, 'you know what you are going to say is likely to annoy me.'

For a few seconds Travis remained silent.

Then he said, 'I asked Sharon to pop round. She phoned me to let me know she still has some of my stuff from the business and she wanted to know the best time to drop it off. So, I suggested she drop it off today and she could stay for a burger and a drink.'

While Travis was talking, I asked myself a series of quick questions. Why did he sound as though he was apologising? What did he expect my reaction to be? What if I said *no*, I don't want her in my house? Although in all honesty I was intrigued.

As I continued to get ready, I said, 'If she wants to pop round, that's fine. I haven't seen her for a while, it will be nice to catch up.'

'I am not saying you have to stop entertaining our other guests to spend time with her,' he said, 'I was letting you know she'd be here.'

I stopped what I was doing and looked directly at him. 'I have nothing against Sharon,' I said. 'The issue was between you and her. So, there is no need for me to be rude and ignore her.'

Travis was stumped for words. He looked as though he wanted to say something further but he wasn't sure what. I suspected that he did not expect my friendly reaction. After a minute or two of not knowing quite what to do, he left the room telling me not to be long because people were arriving. This was clearly his way of trying to control me again and because he told me not to take long, I took my time. As I was sitting in front of the mirror doing my hair, I had one thought and that was; two can play at mental gymnastics! There was a reason Travis informed me that Sharon was going to be at the barbecue and I was determined to do my own investigation to discover the reason.

The barbecue had been underway for about four hours when Sharon arrived. She walked into the garden and I greeted her warmly. 'Hello Sharon, Travis told me you were coming. How are you?'

It was obvious from Sharon's reaction that she was not expecting my warm welcome. In fact, she looked decidedly uncomfortable.

'Hello Melissa,' she said. 'Happy birthday. I am well. Thank you for asking.'

'Would you like to drink?' I asked.

'Thank you,' she said. 'Can I have a ginger ale, please?'

Bella and Simone must have heard me mention Sharon's name when I was greeting her because they seemed to appear suddenly and were standing on either side of me. When I introduced the three of them to each other, Sharon looked even more uncomfortable.

The fact that Travis was not interjecting in my conversation with her led me to believe he did not know Sharon had arrived. This was confirmed when I asked her. 'Have you spoken to Travis yet?'

'No,' she said, 'I only just arrived and walked straight through the back gate.'

No sooner had she finished talking, I saw Travis heading our way. He looked as though he was ploughing through our crowd of guests in his quest to get to us as quickly as possible. It was quite comical and I wanted to laugh out loud. Instead, I turned away and busied myself getting her drink. When he arrived at our little group, he stood beside me and put his arm around my waist. It was difficult to determine if his arm was meant to restrain me from doing or saying anything that could be embarrassing or whether it was to assure Sharon that we were still good.

'Hello Sharon,' he said, 'did you bring the paperwork?'

'Yes,' she responded. 'It's in the car.'

'You had better go and get it,' he said, 'We have a lot more guests coming and I need to be on hand to support Melissa in making sure everybody is catered for.'

As they both walked away, exiting the garden through the back gate, Bella and Simone turned to me and said in unison.

'What the hell was that?'

'That,' I said, 'was Travis making it clear to Sharon she had better not overstay her welcome!'

'Did you invite her?' Simone asked.

'No, Travis did,' I responded. 'He said she had some papers from their closed business she had to drop off and he suggested she did it today.'

'Well, I don't mind telling you,' Bella said. 'I wouldn't have wanted her at my birthday party and she looked guilty as hell!'

'Looking her in the eyes,' I replied, 'I'm not sure the word I would use is guilty, but she definitely looked uncomfortable.'

Within minutes, the papers in hand, Travis made his way back through the garden without Sharon. He walked right up to me and kissed me full on the mouth. That little demonstration of affection, told me two things. One, I was under no illusion that the show was for Bella and Simone and anybody else who was looking on. Two, although I had never directly confronted him about Sharon, he suspected that I knew something had and could still be going on. And more importantly, he suspected that I had shared my suspicions with Bella and Simone.

When he finally let me go, he turned to Bella and Simone and gave them the biggest and brightest smile and said. 'That was to let Melissa know how much I love her.'

He had achieved the desired effect. Both Simone and Bella had melted and were making statements like, 'aww' and 'that's so sweet,' and 'Melissa, you are so lucky to have a man so willing to demonstrate his affection for you in public!'

When he walked away, I turned to Bella and Simone and said, 'After everything I have told you about my suspicions, you should know better than to fall for that little display of his!'

The rest of the day went without any challenges. Everyone enjoyed the food and drinks and the music was so good that several guests danced. The happy birthday salutation went well and I shared my birthday cake. And as usual, by the end of the night, I was exhausted.

When everybody had gone home and Lewis was tucked into bed, Travis and I sat down and had a quiet drink. It was at this point I made the decision to ask the question.

'Travis,' I asked, 'why did you tell me that Sharon was coming here today?'

For a second, I didn't think he was going to answer me. Then he said, 'I don't know. I suppose it was to see what you would say.'

'Now, I am going to ask you outright,' I said, 'Did you have an affair with Sharon?'

'No! I am not saying we didn't fancy each other and we even fooled around a couple of times but it never went as far as sex.'

Genuine interest pushed me to ask the next question.

'If you love me as much as you say you do,' I pushed, 'why did the business relationship you had with Sharon progress to fooling around?'

'I'm not saying this as an excuse,' he replied, 'But it was when we were going through our difficult patch. She was there and it was easy but I did stop myself before it went too far because I love you and I was not going to jeopardise what we have together.'

Thinking consciously, I had no doubt there was some truth in what he said. I was also equally convinced there were lies in the statement too. Reflecting on the choices we make, that night I made the choice to let it go.

****

It was Saturday morning and I was driving home with the food shopping. As I turned into my street, I noticed Travis' car was parked outside the house. The letter I had been waiting for had finally arrived from the university. Instead of leaving it at home – I didn't want Travis to see it – I took the letter with me when I left the house to go shopping. Waiting until I had parked the car, I opened the envelope and read the letter. I had passed the re-sit finance exam! It was hard to keep the smile off my face as I walked through the supermarket. However, the feeling of elation left me because I was hoping Travis would be out with his friends watching football giving me time to relish in my achievement. After parking my car, I walked into the house with the shopping bags. As I closed the door, I heard laughter coming from the lounge. When I put my head round the door, I was surprised to see my two friends, Bella and Simone, sitting comfortably and having a relaxed conversation with Travis.

My first thought was that I didn't remember seeing their cars parked outside. The second thought that struck me was how odd it was for Bella and Simone to be sitting in my lounge because although they were my friends and they knew each other, they were not really that close. And it was strange that they had both arrived at my house at the same time without an invitation from me.

'Darling,' Travis said, as he looked up and saw me standing by the door, 'Look who has come to visit?' His tone was so pleasant. I knew he was up to something. I continued standing looking from him to them and back again.

'Hi you two.' I said by way of a greeting. 'What brings you both to my house on the same day at the same time?'

'Why don't you sit and chat with your friends while I put the shopping away, get you a drink and make lunch?'

He was being so considerate I wanted to puke! I knew the show of offering to put the shopping away – something he rarely did – and suggesting I sit and talk with my friends even though it was lunchtime and Lewis would be hungry was only to impress my girlfriends. When Travis had left the room, I turned to Bella and Simone.

'I don't mean to be rude because I am glad to see you, but what are you both doing here?'

At my direct question, they looked at each other and the look was indication enough that something was going on.

'Well! Spit it out,' I said.

'Why are you refusing to marry Travis, a man who clearly loves and is devoted to you?' Simone said, looking directly at me. 'I wish my man put the shopping away and made lunch.'

I said nothing. Travis had obviously invited them here to put pressure on me. He was also in the house and I felt sure he was eavesdropping.

'I have never known a woman to refuse marriage to a man eager to get married. What is wrong with you?' Bella said.

I said nothing. My silence seemed to give them permission to try and convince me I was making a really big mistake. They started speaking at once and each made it clear that I needed to grasp the opportunity to have a big wedding and stop being stubborn and difficult.

'I haven't had a conversation with either of you about getting married,' I said. 'Why have you turned up today to apply pressure?'

'Travis phoned and said he was having difficulty getting you to agree to walk down the aisle,' Simone said. 'He asked if I could help you make up your mind. I know how stubborn you can be so, I phoned Bella and here we are.'

I was not amused! So now I knew. The pressure was off at home because Travis had adopted a different tactic. Instead of having the arguments and disagreements with me, he had decided to employ the help of my friends to apply peer pressure. The confusion Bella and Simone were feeling regarding my reluctance to get married was clear by the way they were looking at me. Apart from telling them about Sharon, I had not really gone into any depth about how I was feeling about my relationship and the pressure to get married. I really couldn't blame them for thinking they were helping me make my decision.

Interestingly, because the proposal of marriage seemed to be the end of the journey and where all relationships should lead, neither Bella nor Simone had asked why I was reticent. Looking at the two of them sitting in the lounge, I had to admit that at no time had I voiced my concerns about my thoughts or feelings to either of them. Sure, we had conversations about the issues that arise within relationships such as some of the difficulties we have with regards to the excepted roles of the male and female.

We have even had numerous conversations about the strategies we would come up with to get out of having sex when we were not in the mood, but at no time had I mentioned I was avoiding the sanctity of marriage. Given the judgmental looks I was receiving however, keeping the whole issue close to my chest was done with good reason because deep down I suspected the reaction that I was now getting.

The truth was I didn't know how to tell them that although Travis and I were married in all but name I had been sleepwalking my way through the relationship with very little planning on my part. Now that I had woken up, I didn't want to take that final step and be legally bound to him. Convinced Travis was not the man I wanted to marry, I was content with the way I was living until I was ready to leave. Being legally bound through marriage, however, would create an added dimension I didn't need, making the eventual split messy and complicated.

'Look,' said Simone, who had been married for eighteen years, 'everybody goes through the anxiety of getting married. It is normal, but you have a man who absolutely adores you, anybody can see that. He is so concerned you might say *no*, he contacted us to help persuade you. That's love if I ever saw it. Why don't you put him out of his misery and say, *yes*?'

They were both looking at me as though I was being unduly difficult just for the hell of it. From an early age, I was aware my way of thinking was different to many women I knew. So, instead of saying nothing, which was my initial intention, I felt the need to justify my position because it was suddenly important that Bella and Simone did not think of me as different.

'It is not that I don't want to get married,' I responded, 'I do. But I want to get through my college course first. If I start planning a wedding, I think it's going to get in the way. Besides, to be honest, I can't see the rush. We already live together, we have bought a house and we have a child together. The fact that I'm being considered unreasonable because I want to wait until after I have qualified, is a little unfair.'

'We understand where you're coming from,' said Bella who lived with her long-time partner, 'but you don't want to lose him because you are sticking to your guns. Why not set the date and at least that will give him something to work towards?'

I could feel my resolve weakening and before I knew it, I agreed with them.

Travis burst into the lounge, pulled me up off the sofa and hugged me. He turned to Simone and Bella. 'Thank you for getting her to see sense.' I tried to laugh it off, but I knew in that moment I had sealed my fate. It was done and now I had to live with my decision.

Simone and Bella were unaware of the undercurrent. Instead there was an atmosphere of laughter and excitement. Both my friends were already talking about the wedding, the best venues, where to get the wedding dress, what I was going to look like in the dress and who should be invited to the hen night. Throughout the exchange of what, where and when, I was trying to convince myself I had done the right thing.

When Bella and Simone finally left, giving hugs and kisses, I closed the front door and turned to look at Travis.

'Before you start,' he said, 'You left me with no choice. I knew all you needed was a bit of a push and my plan worked. What date shall we set?'

'I have only just agreed to the wedding. Do we have to set the date right now?'

'No, we don't have to set the date right now, but I think the sooner we do, the sooner I can get on and organise things in the background and leave you to get on with your college course.'

I already felt the walls closing in and the pressure to conform making it difficult to breathe. There was only one thought playing over and over again in my mind. *'You've made your bed now you have to lay in it.'*

CHAPTER SEVEN
THE PLANNING

Time: 8:15am; 1 hour 45 minutes left to go

The time I had left – before having to get ready for my wedding – popped back into my consciousness and I did a quick time check. Looking at the clock on the bedside table, I relaxed in the knowledge that I still had time on my side.

I thought about how the pressure increased when even though I had made it clear I wanted to defer the wedding, Travis tried every tactic he could think of to draw me into getting excited about it. Each time I resisted, I saw his brain ticking over as he tried to come up with another angle.

Although I did not have a preference, Travis wanted the wedding to be held on my birthday – my dismay was that this meant my birthday would take second place to our wedding anniversary – but fortunately the venue he had already decided would be the perfect location for the reception was not available and, much to Travis' complete annoyance, the date was set for a month later.

Travis did not waste any time engaging his best man, the ushers and researching for possible caterers. The effort I had to make to resist being caught up and bending to his will was at the expense of the time and energy I needed to complete my dissertation proposal and it was immense. But I was resolute and I would not be deterred. Predictably, I was constantly accused of being selfish and not caring, which often resulted in arguments. It was during this time that Travis admitted he did not want me to succeed in passing this qualification. Even though in the past the thought had crossed my mind, I had dismissed the notion as ridiculous. Hearing the words come out of Travis' mouth confirming my thoughts, however, it was shocking. The admission came out one day when Travis walked into the room and was looking over my shoulder at my computer screen.

'As you are working on your dissertation, I take it you passed your finance exam?' he queried.

'I failed it on the first attempt,' I stated, 'and had to re-sit it.'

'You never said you had failed it!' he accused.

'Since the start of this course,' I challenged, 'I've had the impression you've wanted me to fail and in different ways, you have said as much. I was not going to give you the satisfaction of gloating so, I did the work and passed it the second time.'

'I am not saying I wanted you to fail,' he said. 'I am saying that if you were doing this course to prove that you can, then you've done it. I must admit I did not think you would get this far but you have proved me wrong.'

'But I haven't done it…yet,' I challenged. 'Having done it, would be completing the course and graduating.'

'Why is it so important to you?' he asked. 'We'll be married soon and it will be my job to look after you and our family.'

'What if something happens and you are not around?' I argued. 'I have to be able to look after me and Lewis.'

'That's just it, Melissa,' he responded. 'I'm frightened that when you complete this course, you'll be striving for such heady heights, career wise, it won't be me that won't be here, it will be you.'

'Don't be ridiculous,' I protested. 'You can't seriously want me to drop out and not graduate because you're afraid I will want to improve my career prospects? Isn't that what we all strive for?'

'Don't make me sound stupid, Melissa!' he berated. 'I was only telling you what I thought but if you don't want to take it on board that's up to you!'

Although that was the first time Travis had voiced his fear about how he thought the completing of my university course was going to impact him, I could not deny that he was right. The sole reason for completing the course was to increase my earning capacity so I could leave Travis and live independently. When he left the room, I reflected on the conversation and realised while that was my plan all along, I believed I had hidden it well. Apparently, I had not hidden it well enough and Travis had sensed it. Now I understood his constant encouragement to engage me in the wedding plans. It was in the hope that I'd get so caught up in the planning, that the need to complete my course would be diminished. When that didn't work, Travis baited me with the one thing he knew would be a strong enough argument to hook me.

I remember how every now and then, when the pressure to conform and engage was so out of control, I wanted to scream. Living with Travis for nearly nine years now, I knew once he had made up his mind that he wanted something, he was relentless until he got it. Inviting my best friends into the situation was evidence of that attitude and I couldn't blame Bella and Simone for the state of affairs I found myself in. I knew Travis and they didn't, as they had no idea what they were asking of me, but I did! Consequently, I should never have agreed to the seemingly reasonable suggestion of setting the date.

The day I finally allowed myself to be drawn in came one Saturday during halftime of the football match Travis was watching, when he declared he had a surprise for me.

'What is the surprise?' I enquired.

'Do you remember a couple of years ago when we talked about moving and I said we could not move until I had paid off my credit card debts?' He paused for effect at this point. 'Well, I have done it, so we are now in a position to move if that is what you still want.'

'Okay,' I responded cautiously because I suspected there was more.

'The thing is,' he continued, 'I was thinking it would be great to begin married life with a fresh, new start so if we are going to move, we should try and tie it in with the wedding. That way we can plan the wedding and the house move at the same time.' I was baited and hooked!

When we had bought the three-bed terraced house we were living in, the area wasn't brilliant but for two working adults it was adequate. By the time Lewis came along the area had deteriorated. Violence within some parts of the community – including the massacre in the church – had increased. The streets were unkempt and it was obvious there was a need for a serious injection of financing to improve the community services which included the schools.

Considering the health and wellbeing of Lewis, I was eager to move to a new house in a better area with quieter streets and decent schools. I was also aware that Travis didn't like the upheaval of moving and would have avoided it if he could. Given the need to act quickly to ensure the two activities were being carried out simultaneously, the mammoth task we were taking on did not occur to me. I was simply determined the task would be achieved and so I embraced the opportunity he offered me.

To meet the objective, nine months before the wedding, we made the decision to begin the process of selling the house we lived in and finding somewhere else. Now we were not only planning a wedding, we were also planning to sell our home, buy a new house and move! All my good intentions related to not getting involved went out of the window as I allowed myself to be swept up in a flurry of activity.

Actually, saying that makes it sound like I was just really busy, when in fact, given that we were undertaking two of the top five situations considered to be the most stressful, in anyone's life, and because Travis and I did not work well together at the best of times, it was an absolute nightmare!

Unsurprisingly, when it came to planning the wedding and the hunt for a new house, Travis and I had two different viewpoints. But given our relationship had been based on a series of misconceptions, it should not have been a surprise that we were not on the same page.

When it came to the wedding colours, I wanted purple and ivory for the colour scheme, Travis thought ivory and cream would look better. When sorting out the seating arrangements for the sit-down meal, Travis opposed my thoughts on the subject. He was clear how the tables were going to be arranged and who should be sitting where.

Within three weeks, Travis had given the house a coat of paint, carried out minor repairs and generally prepared the house for sale. While he was doing that, I was furiously working on my dissertation. We contacted a couple of estate agents to evaluate our house. When completed, we were told the house would be on the market within a week and we should start looking for our new home because they expected a quick sale.

We got stuck in straight away and in the week that followed, estate agents were contacted, enquiries were made about available properties for sale and we were added to countless mailing lists. The estate agents selling our house informed us that due to a surge in sales activity, they had been unable to prepare the particulars in time. As a result, our house would not appear in the ***Property Newspaper*** until the following week. I was more than happy with the delay because it gave me a few more days to work on my dissertation. At this point, I was exhausted and most of the time I was eating just enough to keep me going and had forgotten what it was like to get a good night's sleep. But through it all, I refused to give up. It seemed as though I was juggling a number of different balls to within an inch of my life and I was determined – come hell or high water – I was going to keep them in the air for as long as was needed.

One Friday evening, a week before the house went up for sale on the open market, Travis got in from work and called.

'Babe!'

The minute he called me 'babe', I knew he was going to say something I was not going to like.

'Are you alright?' he enquired. 'How was your day?'

'I am fine and my day was good,' I responded, 'What's up?'

'I was speaking with Leroy today and he is feeling a bit stressed and wants to have a short break,' Travis said. 'He asked me to go with him, but I told him I'd have to check with you first.'

I was stunned! Even though he had made his request sound as if I had the final say, we both knew he did not expect me to say anything other than; 'That's fine. You go and enjoy yourself!'

'We are about to start having people view the house,' I responded. 'There will be an expectation that it is constantly kept clean to accommodate potential buyers. And you are asking if you can go on holiday with your friends! When are you supposed to be going?'

'Next Saturday, for a week. I know it is not a good time,' he said. 'But to be honest, Leroy looked depressed and in need of a break. And with all the pressure of organising the wedding and the house hunting, I am exhausted. I thought it would be a good idea to get away for a few days. I told Leroy that depending on what you said, I would contact Paul and Kyle to see if they were up for getting away on a cheap and cheerful break. He was really excited about the idea of a 'guys' holiday.'

I continued looking at him but said nothing. After a while, it was obvious that my lack of a response was beginning to get to him.

'Come on babe. It's not as if we haven't had our family holiday. I thought it would be nice to have some down time, where me and the guys can kick back and relax a bit before the wedding.'

'You mean you want to avoid having to deal with people walking in and out of our house!' I challenged.

When he did not respond immediately, I was about to launch into a tirade of obscenities and tell him how his decision to go on holiday at this time was wrong on so many levels. But as I opened my mouth, I heard myself saying, 'Actually, that's a really good idea. You go on holiday with your friends. That will give us both a break.'

In a lightning flash, I went from being annoyed at his decision to go on holiday with his friends, to thinking, 'This could be good.' I would have a whole week to myself, to relax, catch up with reading research material, hopefully break the back of my dissertation and spend quality time with Lewis.

The guys booked a one-week holiday for Alicante. For the next few days, as much as I tried to hide it, I was almost euphoric. Nothing Travis said could upset me, although I was convinced it was not for the lack of him trying. As the date of his departure drew nearer, Travis began making little remarks about how happy I seemed to be. I was determined not to let anything upset my holiday, so I held my tongue refusing to be drawn in anything he said that was negative. I even had sex without there being an argument about being too tired or not being in the mood.

On the day of his departure, Travis was due to leave the house to make his way to Gatwick airport at 4:30 am. I was really glad when he eventually got out of bed to get ready. Contrary to what he had led me and his friends to believe, Travis hated flying and because of this, he had tossed and turned most of the night. To make matters worse, because he was awake, I was awake.

'Are you going to be okay while I'm away?' he asked.

'We will be fine,' I assured him, 'Don't worry about us, enjoy yourself.'

My one line answers indicating that I was not going to have a full-blown conversation at 1am in the morning were – of course – ignored.

'I know this is not a great time to be taking a break,' he said, 'but it's done now.'

Although he was speaking as though I was complaining and in need of placating, I knew where this conversation was heading. He was angling for sex! It was as though he read my mind because no sooner had the thought popped into my mind than I felt the signature hand on my thigh. Because he had kept me awake, I decided to punish him by taking the emotion out of our coupling. And before he could take the initiation any further I turned on him.

'If all this talk is to keep me awake because you want to have sex, why don't you get on with it? That way, I might be able to get some sleep.'

He removed his hand from my thigh.

'Why can't we have one night when I don't feel as though I am having to fight you for sex?'

I was not going to pander to his hurt feelings.

'That day might happen when you have some consideration for me instead of always putting your own needs first. It is 1am in the morning, you are leaving at 4:30am and when you eventually leave I will have two hours before I must get up and start my day. If you want to have sex, can you get on with it?'

Determined to have his way, we had sex even though it was not an enjoyable experience for either of us. When it was over, I rolled over and went to sleep, leaving him feeling very unsatisfied. Just before I fell asleep, I heard him say something, but I didn't catch it and, quite honestly, I wasn't interested.

Later, I was woken up by a kiss on my cheek. 'I am going now,' Travis said. 'I'll phone you when I get to the hotel.'

'Okay! Have a good trip and I will talk to you soon.'

'I love you,' he said.

'I love you too.' It had been so long since we had said that to each other, it felt odd.

Once I heard him go out the front door, lock it and the slam of the taxi door, the sigh of relief was hard to contain. I thought I would have gone back to sleep. But I felt so excited about the coming week of freedom that it was impossible to sleep. After about thirty minutes, I sat up in bed and switched on the television and watched the news. I marvelled that this was something I would not have been able to do had Travis been here. Within a few minutes, the news faded into the background as for the umpteenth time, I found myself evaluating my relationship and wondering if the problem was him, me, or us together.

What was clear was something wasn't right considering that he had gone on holiday for a week with his friends and instead of being annoyed and upset about it, I was ecstatic!

On the Monday, three days after Travis went on holiday, the house was put on the housing market for sale. I had informed the estate agent that I would do the viewings and had taken a couple of days off work to be available to receive potential buyers. Viewings were booked in to begin on the same day and surprisingly, the second person who viewed the house offered to pay the asking price.

I was feeling pleased with myself and rang Travis to give him the good news.

'Hi, I wanted to let you know I have found a buyer for our house.'

'That's great,' he said. 'Did you get the asking price?'

'The woman said she was going to pay the asking price, but she wanted to talk to her husband first.' I informed him. 'She wants to do another visit with her husband and family.'

'Hmm...that doesn't sound very promising,' he said. 'If the woman hasn't sorted it out with her husband yet, how can you believe her? It sounds like you are getting ahead of yourself.'

As usual, I made the mistake of trying to share good news with Travis and he – as always – found a way of talking to me as though I was a child and had no clue what I was doing. Satisfied he had managed to burst my bubble, he said he had to go and ended the call. For the rest of the evening, although I tried not to think about it, I kept wondering if I was wrong and had misread the enthusiasm I had picked up from the potential buyer with regards to purchasing our house. I went to bed that night convinced I had not misread her excitement and I would find out the following day whether she was serious or not.

The following morning, I received a phone call from the estate agent. They were asking if I would be home after 6pm because the potential buyer from the previous day wanted to arrange for her husband and family to view the house. I busied myself cleaning and preparing for the second visit. At 6pm, the woman turned up with her husband and family. They looked around, asked a few questions and as they were leaving, told me they would contact the estate agent the following day. I made the decision not to inform Travis about the latest development when he rang.

As promised, the buyers contacted the estate agents who contacted me. They liked the house and agreed to pay the asking price. I was over the moon that not only was I right about the family, but I had also sold the house during the week Travis was on holiday and I got the asking price.

'I have sold the house.' I informed Travis when I received my usual phone call that evening.

'Who bought it?' he asked.

'The same woman who said she was going to do a second visit with her husband and family,' I responded.

'When did she make the second visit?'

'Yesterday,' I informed him.

'But I spoke to you yesterday,' he said. 'You didn't say anything about the visit.'

At this point, I could hear the annoyance in his voice and knew this is going to develop into argument if I couldn't head it off.

'Your response was so negative when I mentioned she wanted to make a second visit,' I said. 'I made the decision to be sure before I said anything.'

'That's the problem with you!' he scolded. 'It doesn't matter what my response was, you should have told me!'

'What difference does it make?' I challenged. 'I'm here, you are on holiday, the house is now sold subject to the conveyancing checks and we can get on and find the house we want to buy.'

He was placated for the time being, but I was not fooled. I knew he was not happy and this would come back and bite me. In the meantime, I still had two days of freedom before he returned and I was going to enjoy every minute of it.

Lewis and I went clothes shopping, visited the park, relaxed at home, watched Disney films and played loud music. We knew that the way we were behaving wouldn't last long. Travis was going to be back soon and everything we were doing would have to stop because he liked order and for everything to be neat and tidy. The day before he was due home, I invited Simone and Bella for a girls' night of drinks and a chat. I think I knew at the point of extending the invitation that I was going to be open and honest with them about what I was thinking and feeling.

I bought drinks and nibbles and laid everything out ready for them to arrive at 7pm the doorbell chimed, I went to answer the door. They had both arrived at the same time.

'Great!' I said by way of a greeting, followed by hugs and kisses on the cheek.

'Come in and make yourself at home.'

When Bella and Simone were seated and comfortable, I poured each of us a glass of wine and we indulged in some nibbles. The conversation was light and frivolous and for about an hour we were laughing and giggling.

'Why did you invite us here this evening?' asked Simone suddenly.

I looked at them both and knew it was now or never.

'I invited you here tonight,' I began, 'because I wanted to have a free and open conversation with you both before Travis gets back from his holiday.'

'Is everything alright?' Bella asked.

'When Travis invited you here to help me make up my mind about getting married,' I began, 'he felt he had to employ underhanded tactics because he knew I didn't want to get married. And in truth, I don't think it's that I don't want to get married, I don't think I want to marry him!'

Bella and Simone looked dumbstruck.

'What do you mean you don't want to marry him, he loves you?' Simone said. 'Are you sure you're not just being your usual stubborn self?'

I looked down at my feet and then looked at each of them in turn and burst into tears. They saw me as a strong character who was phased by very little. For a minute or two, neither knew quite what to do with me crying. Bella was spurred into action first.

'Whatever is the matter?' she asked as she hugged me.

I didn't know where to start and so, I said nothing and continued crying. After a few minutes, I managed to compose myself. I dried my eyes, took a big gulp of wine and tried to organise my thoughts.

'I don't think I can marry Travis,' I said. 'I think he will make my life hell if I do. On the surface, he is one thing and people like him. God! You two think he is great. But underneath.... there is something! I don't think I can cope with this other side of him.'

'What do you mean, underneath he is something else?' Bella said, raising her voice. 'Whenever we come around for parties and gatherings, all we ever see is someone who is attentive, helps out, only ever has nice things to say about you and adores you.'

'That is just it,' I responded. 'When he is being observed, he is all the things you say and at first I was taken in by it. But when we are alone, there is a controlling side to him that I am constantly battling. It gets so bad at times, I feel as though I'm tearing my hair out. To make matters worse, whenever we have a disagreement, it is usually because I am refusing to bend to his will and when this happens, he blames me for the contention within our relationship.'

I saw from the look on Simone and Bella's face that I had done a good job of hiding the concerns I had about my relationship.

'I don't know what to say,' said Bella. 'You always look so happy together. Are you sure it is as bad as you say or do you think it is pre-wedding jitters? I mean, you must know how bad it is and I don't mean to diminish what you have said, but surely you can work this out!'

'Look,' said Simone. 'It sounds as if you are saying that you want out. But I must ask you to think before you do anything you might regret. You have a son together. You wouldn't want him to grow up in a single parent household? You also have a lovely home and a man who loves you, even if he might be a bit controlling. It is a fact that most women have to compromise in their relationship. Find a way to create a situation where you understand each other better, rather than giving up everything you have worked for!'

'I agree with Simone,' said Bella. 'Travis is a man's man and most women like that. It is just that you are headstrong and refuse to be dominated. Come on, you have got to find a way to get past this.'

'I don't know how I can get past it,' I responded. 'If Travis is determined to dominate me and I refuse to be dominated, what kind of life is that?'

'If you ask me,' Simone said, wiggling her eyebrows, 'it makes for an exciting life!'

We laughed at her insinuations and just as she had intended, the conversation dissolved into talking about sex. By the end of the evening, I was feeling better. The nibbles were all gone, the two wine bottles were empty and I asked Simone if she would be my maid of honour. I had even convinced myself that my concerns were all in my head and I had magnified the situation. By the time I got into bed, I had an increased determination to try and improve my relationship. Travis was due home the following afternoon and for the first time, I was not dreading his return.

―― CHAPTER EIGHT ――

WHAT HAPPENS BEHIND CLOSED DOORS...

Time: 9am; 1 hour 00 minutes left to go

Returning my thoughts to the present, I turned and looked at the clock. I had an hour left before I had to start getting ready. I had been lying here musing for three hours! It really didn't seem that long. Even though it was unlikely, I did a quick internal assessment of my body, checking my need for the toilet. Unlike many mothers who suffer from having a weak bladder when they have children, I can go hours without needing to use the toilet, even if everyone I know keeps telling me it is not healthy. I was getting thirsty however and wondered if I should get myself another drink. Apart from being too lazy to get up, I was running out of time and thinking about the trek to the kitchen. Waiting for the kettle to boil, making the tea and returning to my bedroom with it, not only seemed like too much hassle, but it would eat into the hour I had left!

I had covered a great deal of ground and made some good headway, but I wasn't finished and I was determined to conclude my reflective analysis. Besides, the hairdresser was due in about an hour and I would be able to get a drink before she did my hair. With the decision made to go without another drink, I relaxed and settled my mind.

Thinking back to the conversations I had with Bella and Simone allowed me to get back into the reflective zone and all my analytical thoughts returned in a rush. I couldn't help thinking that if I had been more discerning about the warning signals I avoided all those years, I would not be in the situation I was now; about to get married and dreading it! No matter which way I looked at it – ignoring the fact that I had compromised more than I should have – I had given Travis the impression that he did not have to be mindful of my feelings or what I wanted.

By bending to Travis' needs and ignoring my own, I let him believe I didn't matter. As a result, decisions such as planning a holiday, choosing a new dining table or deciding where to eat out, were all organised according to what he wanted.

It could be argued that I had made such a song and dance about not wanting to be involved in the wedding planning, I should not have been annoyed when decisions were being made without my views being considered. I didn't think this meant the colour scheme and the music we were going to dance to and everything in between would be organized with little regard for whether I agreed or not. On the few occasions when I did disagree with his decision, it resulted in an argument, so eventually I stopped making suggestions and let him get on with it.

Having to accept that I allowed Travis to have his own way with regards to the planning of the wedding, left a bad taste in my mouth and a knotted feeling in the pit of my stomach. This was due to the realisation that in tolerating his behaviour, I gave Travis the permission to emotionally abuse me. I felt my anger rising, but on a rational level, I knew if I wanted to complete my analytical journey, getting angry now would get in the way. But realising the part I had played in arriving at my current situation left me wanting to cry. Reigning in my emotions, I gave myself a mental kick and refused to give in to the self-pity. Taking a few deep breaths to calm myself down, I returned to the memory of when Travis returned home from his holiday.

I had woken up early and made sure the house was clean and tidy. I had cooked a meal and mentally prepared myself for Travis' return. While cooking and cleaning, the old adage, **'Absence makes the heart grow fonder'**, popped into my thoughts. However, reflecting on the conversation with Bella and Simone the night before, I had a hard time accepting the idea of being dominated. When Travis and I first met, my perception was that we were equals and that notion had never changed. To accept being dominated was difficult to comprehend. But listening to the views of my friends, it was as though there was some kind of unwritten law stating that, being the woman, it was expected that I adopt a secondary role within a relationship.

I wondered if the problem between Travis and I really was rooted in the fact that I refused to be dominated. During our years together, there had certainly been indications that as the male, he thought of himself as superior. When I had resisted his perceived superiority, it always ended in an argument. I now had to consider what I was going to do because I was clear that being dominated did not work for me! What I was prepared to do, however, was compromise a little more. When Travis walked through the door, I was genuinely pleased to see him.

As we hugged and kissed each other, he asked, 'Did you miss me?'

'Of course, I did,' I responded.

'Good,' he said.

At his response, I thought, **here we go**! I was either going to react to his sanctimonious statement or let it go. If I was going to follow through on my decision to try and compromise to improve our relationship, I needed to start now. He looked surprised when I did not respond to his off-handed statement, but said nothing. The rest of the evening was spent with him telling me the highlights of his holiday and asking about the sale of the house and what we needed to do next.

We planned to contact the estate agents we had registered with, letting them know we had sold our house and they needed to put us on their priority list. We also made the decision to focus our weekends on driving around to choose the area we wanted to live in. During the planning, I made every effort to compromise where necessary and not disagree too often. It would be a falsehood to state we had no disagreements, but the strategy seemed to work as we disagreed less and communicated more.

Once the plan was in place, life was hectic for the next few weeks. I am not sure how I managed it, but in between my job, being a mother, planning the wedding, (of which I was slowly being sucked into) and meeting Travis' physical and emotional demands, as well as house hunting, I found the time to work on my dissertation and was on the home stretch to completing it. This meant life was pretty full on!

My friends kept trying to get me to look around for a suitable wedding dress, but I kept putting it off, refusing to hunt for a dress until I had completed my dissertation.

A month later, not only had I finally completed my dissertation, we had also found the house we wanted to buy. It was a four-bedroom semi-detached, with an integral garage and a driveway big enough to accommodate two cars. It was a fixer-upper with a fair amount of work to do to bring the house up to the living standards we wanted. However, we made an offer and, after a fair amount of negotiating, the offer was accepted.

Then our challenges really started because I was familiar with the buying and selling process and although I did not like to follow convention, I fell into the assumption that I would organise the wedding and Travis would be responsible for managing the house purchase.

Travis, however, was not as familiar with buying and selling houses and he didn't like not having control of the process. He constantly fretted about our buyers pulling out and the impact that would have on our ability to exchange contracts in time for the wedding. He engaged me in long conversations – designed to settle this anxiety – but these left me exhausted because if I said anything that indicated a problem, he fixated on it. He drove me mad!

Given Travis' tendency to be controlling, I was not sure why I thought he would handle the buying of the house situation differently. One evening, having listened to the latest anxiety ridden rant about not hearing from the estate agent or receiving information about the outcome of the surveyor's report, I'd had enough and we had a huge argument.

'Planning the wedding is my responsibility and the purchase of the house is your responsibility,' I stated, rather loudly. 'Why do you keep asking me about what is happening with the house purchase when you should be keeping on top of it?'

Without uttering a word, he looked to me for a least a minute.

'If you want me to be honest,' he began. 'I think we should have a serious conversation about our strengths to determine who should be doing what!'

'What do you mean *who should be doing what*?' I restated.

'I have always had a vision of how my wedding was going to be,' Travis said. 'And let's be honest Melissa, you don't have a clue.'

Then to my surprise, he said, 'You know what? I think it would be easier if you organised the house purchase, deal with the lawyers and the estate agents and leave me to deal with the wedding. I am much better at planning than you are anyway.'

For a second, I was really annoyed. Travis had given me a backhanded compliment because he could not admit he was unable to cope with the uncertainties of the selling and buying process.

He must have seen – by the look on my face – that I was gearing up to absolutely disagree with him. But before I could respond, he continued in a more conciliatory tone.

'Look Melissa, all I am saying is that we both have different strengths and with everything that is going on, it is time to play to those strengths. You can manage and cope better than I can with lots of different things without getting stressed or angry. And I am better at detail than you are. It would make more sense if we swapped roles. I know everybody thinks it should be the woman who plans and organises the wedding and the man's role to manage the house buying but in this relationship, it would work better the other way around.'

'Okay!' I said, without conviction, 'I suppose that makes sense and as you put it that way. I agree. Let's swap!'

Irritated that Travis had placed his ability to organise and deal with detail, above my ability to organise and deal with complex situations, was the reason I had given him a response lacking enthusiasm. But secretly, I was so relieved he was taking over the planning of the wedding. It felt amazing to have the worry and the stress that I didn't even know I was feeling, just disappear. When I analysed why that was, it became clear that I didn't have to worry about getting the planning of Travis' wedding wrong.

'Oh!' he said, 'We don't need to tell anybody we have swapped roles!'

That last statement was a dig, letting me know that he would not be telling anyone and I should do the same. In other words, I should not tell Bella or Simone. Even though Travis had come up with the idea, it was apparent that he was embarrassed about not being able to do the 'manly thing' and wanted me to assure him that I would be complicit in the ploy if anyone asked. The old saying; **'What happens behind closed doors'**, came to my mind.

At that thought, the speed at which I left my memories and was back in the present, made my head spin. Why wasn't I strong enough to say from the outset that this was not going to work out? If I was getting stressed about getting the wedding planning wrong, what was going to happen when the real difficulties arose? I also thought about the swap in roles. In the great scheme of things, it looked like a minor issue. But, in reality, the smoke and mirrors concocted to present an ideal picture image to friends and family was the crux of our relationship. Each time I compromised and agreed with the ploy, I allowed myself to be sucked further into a way of being that took something away from my moral values.

I sat up in bed and again focused on my wedding dress and, not for the first time while I had been reflecting, all I could think was; **'Oh my god, what have I done? This is going to be a nightmare. This marriage is a mistake!'**

As I continued to look at my wedding dress, I asked myself why I had made the decision to say *yes* to marriage when the man I am marrying lived by such a different moral code to me. It was inevitable that my life would be miserable. I had done a great deal of reflecting while thinking about my journey to this point. And although there were revelations I didn't know were lurking in my subconscious – not being able to truthfully answer the question about why I said *yes* to Travis – meant I had not gone to the core of the matter. I suspected it was because I didn't want to face it. But it was now or never. If I didn't face the reason for making my decision now, I knew myself well enough to know the answer could occur at the most inappropriate of times, such as, while standing at the alter preparing to say, 'I do!' There was no more room for ignoring the truth. I needed the answer and I needed it now!

Before allowing myself the time to delve back into my subconscious, I checked the time. My family would be arriving in three hours. The time check indicated I could spare a few more minutes to think about why I had made my decision.

I could convince myself that it was peer pressure, but I knew myself well enough to know that I didn't bow to peer pressure easily. Especially if it was something I really didn't want to do. So that couldn't be it.

As I was peeling back the layers, I knew the reason for my decision was related to a need that I had failed to recognise on a conscious level. In the safety of my bedroom, where everything emotionally harmful was outside, I travelled deeper into my subconscious allowing myself to be as open and as vulnerable as was necessary to get to my truth.

And then, my truth began to emerge. Although I didn't want to be locked into a marriage with Travis, I did want to know what it would feel like to walk down the aisle. I also knew the need that I had, was not my need, but a duty I felt I owed to my mother, who had never been married and believed she was unlucky when it came to the men in her life. She never accepted that being denied the opportunity to have her special day was due to her choice of men.

She got on well with Travis and often referred to him as the kind of man she would have wanted to marry when she was young. When the realisation hit me, I opened my eyes with a start and looked up at the ceiling. And then I began to reiterate my thoughts on a conscious level.

I was getting married to a man whose moral values were not the same as mine because I wanted to prove to myself that I was not unlucky with men. I also wanted to prove to my mother that her life's disappointments did not apply to her children. It was amazing how all that negative stuff I had heard from my mother during my childhood had stuck with me, even though I didn't think it had. I was not blaming my mother for the decision that I had made but I did acknowledge I had cloaked myself in the negative views she had of her life being a single parent with four children.

I had already started on that path. I had one child and even though I wasn't a single parent, in that I lived with my child's father, I still wasn't married. And even though I might not stay married, my subconscious was telling me that walking down the aisle would be the beginning stage of breaking the belief I had picked up from my mother.

It also began to emerge that although I was not completely happy with Travis, I stayed with him to prove to myself that it could be done and I was different to my mother because I could sustain a long-term relationship. The problem was that any way I looked at it I was making decisions not based on what I wanted, but based on childhood perceptions. This revelation was the mother of them all, because it meant that I had to take responsibility for my own life and make decisions according to what I wanted. No longer could I subconsciously blame someone else for my actions.

Having a deeper understanding of what had driven my behaviour allowed me to think more clearly about the compromises I had been making without admitting it to myself. For years, I had been telling myself – even though Travis and I were living together – that I was my own person and he could not tell me what to do. Thinking back to the purchase of my wedding dress, I knew I had been lying to myself and it was time to confess to the truth.

CHAPTER NINE

THE STRAW THAT BROKE THE CAMEL'S BACK

Time: 9:30am; 00 hours 30 minutes left to go

A month after completing my dissertation, Bella, Simone and I went shopping for a suitable wedding dress. We had done our research to find the best place with a full range of dresses reasonably priced.

On the day we arranged to meet, I drove to the shop armed with two wedding magazines. Once inside the shop, I opened the magazines to the pages that had been folded back. Bella looked at the magazines and said, 'When did you buy these? I didn't think you would be this prepared especially as we had to drag you here!'

Bella took the magazines out of my hand, looked at the pages that were folded and then showed them to Simone. Both agreed they liked the dresses that were marked and asked me why I had chosen those particular designs. I remembered looking at the two of them and asking myself if I should tell them the truth or lie. If I told them the truth, I would be going back on the pact I made with Travis about not telling anybody we had switched roles. But if I lied, I would have to remember the lie if it ever came up in the future.

I made the decision to tell them the truth. 'I didn't buy the magazines, Travis did. He looked through them and marked out the two pages suggesting that if I got something that was a cross between the two, he would be happy.'

The response I got was expected. For a minute or two, there was total silence. Then they both started speaking at the same time, asking me if I was crazy.

'Why would you allow Travis to choose the style of dress you are going to wear on your wedding day?' they asked.

I shrugged off the questions, saying that it didn't matter and that I liked the dresses but deep down I was embarrassed and knew they were right. When Travis gave me the magazines with the pages already folded, I asked him why he had done that. He said it was because they were the ones he liked and that it wasn't just my day, it was his day as well and he wanted me to look nice. I was really annoyed because he was telling me he didn't trust my judgement to buy something that was nice. Deep down, I think I also agreed he had better taste than I did. However, I knew that if I confronted him, it would cause an argument. For that reason, I said nothing.

My friends were very discreet and said nothing more about my style of wedding dress being chosen by Travis, but I could tell they were not happy with my answer. As we walked around the shop, I heard them talking among themselves and making statements, such as; 'I would never allow the man I was going marry to choose my wedding dress!' and 'Who does he think he is? What a cheek!'

I did not stop them from making the comments because deep down I agreed, but I didn't want to admit it. Instead, I convinced myself they were entitled to their own opinion. Both Bella and Simone could see that I had disengaged from the activity. To make the best of the situation, they tried to get me into the spirit of choosing a suitable dress, but it was too late and the damage was done. As I walked around the shop, all I was asking myself was; 'Why? Why did I allow him to control what I was going to wear on the day?' While I was musing, my friends got the attention of the woman serving in the store and asked her if she had any dresses that looked like the ones marked in the magazines.

The woman in the shop went across to a rack of dresses and started sifting through them. After about three minutes, she picked up a long rod with a hook on the end that was placed beside her and pulled down three dresses. She suggested that I go into the changing room and try them on. When I tried on the first one, I didn't like it much, but I did begin to get into the swing of things. The second one didn't fit me properly, but the third one was absolutely delightful. It was at that moment that I knew I had not argued with Travis because I would not have had a clue what to buy. I wanted to feel like a princess and if he chose the dress, I wouldn't have to worry that he would be disappointed by my choice.

All the doubts and misgivings about the wedding began to disappear as I stepped out of the changing room and saw the look of amazement on the faces of my two friends. They made enthusiastic statements like; 'Amazing!', 'You look fantastic!' and 'That dress is really you!' And, at that moment, I felt really special. The woman in the shop made the required alterations and told me she would give me a ring when the dress was ready for collection.

When my friends and I stepped out of the shop, they were still gushing about the wedding dress I had chosen and excited about the next leg of our shopping spree. The next step was to buy all the trimmings to go with it. I have never really enjoyed clothes shopping, so the thought of having to go and buy shoes, underwear and jewelry, filled me with dread. We made a date to do the rest of the shopping and they dropped me off at home. As I stepped into the house, Travis asked me whether I had chosen a dress. When I said I did, he asked me what it was like. I told him it was somewhere in between the two dresses that he had chosen in the magazines. He looked satisfied, but then he ruined my sense of peace when he said, 'I am glad you asked Bella and Simone to go with you. They at least would make sure you got something halfway decent!'

And there it was! That constant putting me down and making me aware that my role was to please him. That one statement was the straw that broke the camel's back and I decided enough was enough and the challenge was on. I was not going to let that statement slide. When I asked him what he meant by that, he was a bit taken aback because I had been letting him get away with little statements like that for weeks. He realised too late that he had gone too far and we were going to argue and we certainly did. We didn't speak for a week!

During this particular 'Cold War' period, I had shopped for the shoes to match the dress and the underwear to ensure all my lumps and bumps were tucked in to give the dress that smooth look and the long silk gloves to finish off the ensemble.

Then, surprisingly for the first time following a period of no speaking, Travis tried to apologise, giving me an explanation that he did not mean to be disrespectful but he was feeling the pressure of making sure everything went according to plan. The house move had ten people in the chain. The pressure I was under, being responsible for and having to keep on top of all that while providing him with regular updates, didn't enter his head. I didn't have it in me to go another round and I let it go.

As the date of the wedding drew nearer, I was getting more and more anxious and the more anxious I was getting, the more detached I became. My friends asked me what jewelry I was wearing and my response was, 'I don't know. I'm sure I can find something in my jewelry box.'

On one occasion, when I was in a particularly detached mode, my friends asked me what was wrong. I opened my mouth and instead of saying the truth, that I wasn't sure about the wedding, nor about the marriage and I didn't want to do this and felt as though I was being coerced into doing something I wasn't ready for, I didn't. In the blink of an eye, I made the decision to lie and said, 'I'm just a bit tired with all the stress of the planning.'

As expected from friends, they had the usual statements on hand for when the bride-to-be was exhibiting stress.

'It is usual to feel this way before your wedding,' Simone said. 'You will be fine, we are here for you.'

I let it go. But I could have kicked myself for not telling the truth about how I was feeling. I was actually shutting down my emotions more and more and becoming detached was the only way to deal with my sense of being overwhelmed.

A few days later, I received a phone call from Travis with a demand not a request.

'Contact the estate agent and find out if there are any issues we need to be aware of because I want to make sure we get to move the week after we get married!'

I was busy at work and furious that he expected me to drop everything to address his anxiety. Life was already stressful without having additional pressure to deal with. I got quite annoyed on the phone, letting him know I was busy and reminded him that he was sorting out the wedding and my responsibility was to sort out the house move. I was greeted with silence. Ending the call, I knew I had a headache situation to look forward to when I got home.

'I work too so don't talk to me as if your job is more important than mine,' was the statement I walked into when I arrived home that evening. Overworked and feeling as though my head was going to explode, I let rip.

'You expect me to fail at sorting this out, don't you?' I accused. 'Remember, it was your idea to swap roles. And even though you made the decision, it grieved you that you couldn't handle the stress of dealing with the many variables of selling and buying and you had to hand it over to me!'

'Don't be ridiculous,' he stated in an offhand way. 'I just want to make sure that we move a week after the wedding that's all I'm asking.'

'What do you mean *that's all you're asking*?' I challenged. 'I don't have control of making sure the ten people in the chain have all sorted out their mortgage and have had their evaluations done. To make matters worse, I have already told you that half the chain has engaged conveyancing and the other half has engaged lawyers. This has made communication difficult because the lawyers don't always speak to the conveyancers.'

'Oh!' he said. 'I don't remember you telling me that before.'

'I did tell you,' I shot back, 'but you were obviously not listening.'

'Just to clarify,' he said, 'I don't expect you to fail. This is what you are good at because you have more patience than I do and I know it will be fine. I just don't like not being able to force the process that's all.'

Coming from Travis, that admission was praise indeed and I accepted it graciously without making any further comment.

'Remember we are going to choose the wedding car at 1pm tomorrow,' he went on. 'And, if you are going shopping, make sure you are not late getting back.'

Why he had to tag that last sentence onto the end of his statement was one of the things I could not stand about him. It was his way of making sure I complied with his command. What was even more annoying was the fact that he knew if I was working to a timeline, I was never late.

Even though I was still apprehensive about the wedding, I was looking forward to choosing the limousine I wanted from the wedding car service.

The following day, before going to choose the car, the morning was taken up with washing, cooking and cleaning; the usual chores for a Saturday morning. Lewis was playing with his friend next door and the parents agreed to look after him until we got back. At 12:30 pm, we set off to the wedding car service. I had expectations that we were going to pull up in front of a big car showroom with lots of limos to choose from. Instead, Travis parked in front of a small car lot, with a few cars – nice though they were – none of them looked like a limousine.

Before getting out of the car, I turned and looked at him.

'What?!' he said.

'Out of all the wedding car services available, why did you choose this one?' I asked.

'I chose this one because it wasn't too large,' he said, 'and I thought they could do us a good deal. I know it doesn't look like much, but let's go and see what they've got on offer.'

As we got out of the car and I waited for him to lock up, I happened to see the expression on his face before he was able to put his game face on. Something about the look left me with no illusions. Suddenly, my expectations plummeted when I realised he must have done some kind of deal with this car service and I was not going to get to my limousine.

'How many more times am I going to have to learn this lesson?' I asked myself, *'You should know by now that your needs don't count. The only thing that matters is that he gets what he wants and is happy because he thinks for both himself and for you.'*

As we walked towards the reception office, my suspicions were realised when a salesman walked towards us with his hands outstretched. He had a big smile on his face and greeted Travis by his first name. Looking at the interaction, I wanted to scream.

Travis was about to introduce me to the salesman but he made the mistake of looking at me at the same time. The look on my face must have said it all – because there was an ever so slight hesitation – before the introductions were made.

He knew that I knew!

'Thomas,' Travis began, 'meet Melissa, the woman I'm going to marry!'

Thomas turned to me and said, 'You are the lucky lady who has captured the big guy's heart?'

Hmm, confirmation! I thought. There is too much familiarity. They know each other. I plastered a smile on my face, but said nothing.

'We are looking for a really nice car for our wedding day,' said Travis. I noticed he didn't say a limousine. 'What kind of a deal can you do for us?'

Thomas enthusiastically told us he could do a great deal on a car and as we began to walk across to the parked cars, Travis placed his hand on the small of my back. This was an action he made when he was silently indicating that I take on the role of the 'little lady', which meant be quiet, behave and let him do the talking.

Travis and Thomas started talking about what was available and every now and then one or the other would try to bring me into the conversation, asking my opinion. Each time I shrugged my shoulders or looked vacant as though I had no clue what they were talking about.

After a while, Travis began to feel uncomfortable as I distanced myself from the conversation. I began to understand he wanted me to gush at each suggestion or plead to have a closer look as each car was presented. Each time I said nothing.

When the selection of cars available had been exhausted, Travis turned to Thomas and suggested he give us a few minutes to decide. As Thomas left us and was out of earshot, Travis turned to me and said, 'What is wrong with you? Thomas has showed us some really nice cars and you have not shown interest in any of them.'

At this point I'd had enough with the charade.

'When we started looking for wedding cars,' I challenged, 'you asked me what I wanted and I said I wanted a limousine. There are no limousines in this car lot!'

'Look,' he said, 'I was thinking that everybody has limousines when they are getting married; why not do something different? The Bentley we looked at was really nice. Let's look at it again. I think that would be great for our wedding. It's different and looks more expensive than a limo.'

We walked towards the Bentley, opened the back doors and climbed in the back of the car where we settled into the comfortable leather seats.

'This is lovely,' Travis gushed, trying to convince me it was a better choice than a limo. I had lost interest in the car we were going to hire because I couldn't get my head past the level of manipulation I had been subjected to. He sensed my less than enthusiastic responses to his overexcited constant chatter. But it was obvious he did not want me to say anything so he made the decision not to call me on it. Instead, he carried on talking.

'I think we should talk to Thomas about hiring the Bentley,' he said after a few minutes of bouncing up and down on the leather seats and checking out the interior from our position in the back of the vehicle. I said nothing and because I wasn't disagreeing, he took this to mean I had accepted his decision.

'I have convinced her this is the perfect car for our wedding,' Travis said when Thomas walked back towards the car to see if we had made a decision.

'Great!' said Thomas on hearing the news, 'You will not be sorry. This is one of the most comfortable and reliable cars in our collection. I've never had a complaint about this one.'

We left the car hire service thirty minutes later, once we had returned to the office and signed the required forms.

'How do you know Thomas?' I asked on the drive home.

Following an ever so slight hesitation, Travis said, 'I don't really know him. When I put the word out that I was looking for a wedding car service with reasonably priced cars, Thomas was recommended and I thought I would check him out.' The slight hesitation in answering the question told me everything I want to know. He was lying.

'You knew there were no limousines available before we arrived didn't you!' I accused.

'I am not sure why you are so fixated on having a limousine,' he said, failing to answer my question. 'The Bentley is classier and we got a good deal.'

'It is amazing how you do that,' I said. 'The issue here isn't the limousine versus the Bentley. It is the fact that you withheld the truth which, I suspect, is that you had already contacted the car hire service we have just visited and knew the car I wanted was not available.'

'I didn't tell you about this car hire service because I knew what you would say. I thought it would be better if we came and had a look together. But as usual, even though we found a better car, you are complaining because you can't help yourself, can you?'

And here we went again. He had screwed up. I had called him out on it and now he was doing his best to turn the tables to make it look as though we were arguing because of something I had done. We sat in uncomfortable silence for the rest of the journey home because I refused to bend and was determined he was going to admit he had tried to pull the wool over my eyes.

'Look, I am sorry you never got the car that you wanted,' he said as we pulled up outside our house. 'I tried my best, but limousines are popular cars and I couldn't find a place that was hiring at a reasonable price.'

Shocked, didn't quite sum up my reaction to his apology.

'Why didn't you simply tell me the truth in the first place?' I asked.

'I thought you would have been stubborn and held out for the limousine,' he said, while having the good grace to look a little sheepish.

I let the issue drop because of his apology. And for the first time in weeks, the rest of the weekend passed without incident.

The date was set for everyone in the housing chain to exchange keys one week after the wedding. I was feeling very excited about the move. I contacted the schools in the area of our new house; I notified the post office of our move and I registered with the usual services and facility providers.

Most of the time I did a good job of managing the needs of Travis and Lewis: while wedding invitations were written; the house was kept clean; wedding caterers were secured; the washing and ironing was done; the wedding rehearsals were arranged; the groceries were bought and the food was cooked. What I was not so good at hiding was my frustration at the expectation that I was supposed to manage the added pressure. Rarely did Travis ask me how I was doing or offer any help. This resulted in me biting my tongue most of the time and keeping silent!

With so much going on, I felt exhausted too. One Friday evening, a week and one day before the wedding, I had collected Lewis from nursery on the way home from work. We were entering the house and I wondered where Travis was and what to do for dinner, when my mobile phone started buzzing. I thought it was Travis letting me know he was going to be late but when I looked at the caller identity, it was Simone.

'Hi, Simone. How are you doing?' I said.

'Melissa! I've been trying to get hold of you,' Simone responded.

'I was driving and I didn't hear the phone ringing. What's the matter?' I asked.

'There's nothing wrong. I know you have a lot going on and I wanted to remind you about your hen night, tomorrow.'

'I haven't forgotten Simone. But to tell you the truth, I'm so tired, I don't know if I can muster up the energy!'

'I knew you would say that,' Simone said. 'That is why I am ringing you. It is your hen night so, it is going to look a bit odd if you are not there! Look, to make it a bit easier on you, I am going to pick you up so you won't have to worry about driving.'

I was about to answer Simone, when I saw there was an incoming call on my phone. It was Travis. I knew I had better answer it because he hated it when he called me and I didn't answer immediately.

'Simone, Travis is trying to get hold of me. Let me find out what he wants and I'll ring you right back!'

'Okay,' Simone said, 'get back to me when you have finished talking to him?'

'Hello Travis, where are you?'

'Why did it take you so long to answer the phone?' he responded.

I was not in the mood for his nonsense and my initial thought was to answer him using what he referred to as my 'superior' voice knowing it was bound to cause an argument. Deciding not to fall into the trap, I took a deep breath before responding.

'I was talking to Simone about my hen night tomorrow evening.'

'Hmm....I don't remember you telling me it was tomorrow?'

'Well, I clearly remember telling you,' I said, 'And Bella was there at the time.'

'That means I am going to have to look after Lewis for the evening. You should have reminded me if I had something to do tomorrow evening.'

'How can you refer to looking after your son like it is such a chore? Look, if you don't want to look after him tomorrow that's fine. I'll have to find somebody else because it is my hen night and I will be going.'

'Don't put words into my mouth. I didn't say I don't want to look after Lewis. What I said was, you didn't remind me and I could have organised something else tomorrow. Besides, who else could you find to babysit for the evening? I take it all the friends we normally call on to babysit, are going to be at your hen night. It looks like I don't have a choice but to stay home tomorrow night, doesn't it?'

After ten years of being in a relationship with Travis, I knew when he wasn't happy and was trying to pull me into an argument. However, I made the decision that I was not going to be drawn in. After his explosive statement about having to stay home, I said nothing. After a minute of silence on the phone he said, 'Right, it looks like I'm staying home tomorrow night. You better get back to Simone to finalise the arrangements.'

The last statement was to let me know that the only reason I was going to my hen night the following evening was because he was allowing it. By not arguing with him, he was satisfied that I understood the importance of complying with his wish to be given priority consideration in all things and being allowed to attend my own hen night without more of a fuss, given the inconvenience to him, was my reward!

'I'll talk to you later,' was my response.

'Oh yes! I remember why I rang you now,' he said. 'I'm going out for a drink with the lads. I won't be late.'

'Bye,' I said and ended the call.

Even though I had managed to stay calm during the conversation with Travis, by the time I had redialled Simone's number I was furious.

'Hi Simone, what time are you picking me up tomorrow evening?'

'What's the matter, Melissa?' Simone asked. 'You sound really pissed off. Are you and Travis arguing again?'

I didn't want to discuss my annoyance but I couldn't help myself. 'That fucking man I am going to marry is the matter!' I almost shouted.

'Why? What has happened?'

'What has happened is that I am going to my hen night tomorrow evening and I forgot to remind him and he was not best pleased. He said, I should have reminded him because he could have had something organised for tomorrow evening and now he has got to babysit!'

'You are joking?' Simone said.

'I wish I was,' I replied.

'Listen,' Simone said diplomatically, 'You are both feeling the stress and pressure of the wedding next week. You need a good night out to relax and enjoy yourself. Everything will be alright. You'll see. I will pick you up at 7:30pm tomorrow evening. Leave everything to me.'

I decided to allow Simone to lead me to a more positive place in my thoughts instead of the place of negative thinking I was in before I phoned her back.

When I ended the call with Simone, I was feeling much better. I organised dinner for Lewis and myself and left some for Travis when he got home later. Lewis and I spent the evening chatting and playing until I put him to bed at 7:30 pm.

Travis was home by 9:30 pm. He seemed to be in a better mood then when we were on the phone earlier in the evening.

'Did you have a good evening?' I asked when he was sitting down eating what I had cooked earlier.

'It was all right,' he replied. 'The lads at work wanted to take me out for the drink to celebrate our wedding. It was a good job I decided to go tonight instead of tomorrow though, wasn't it?'

'Let's not bring that up again,' I said. 'We have been through this already when we were on the phone earlier. It is not as if I didn't tell you the hen night was tomorrow! Yes, I might not have reminded you, but when we were discussing the hen and stag nights, we did agree that it was not possible for the two of us to be out on the same night because one of us would need to be at home to care for Lewis. As you were going to have your stag night the day before the wedding, I would have my hen night the week before. And as this is the only weekend, between now and the wedding, it must be tomorrow.'

'Hmm… I am not saying you should not go to your hen night,' Travis said. 'What I am saying, is that you should have reminded me.'

I saw Travis was not going to let it go and that if I carried on with this conversation, it was going to dissolve into yet another argument which is what tended to happen when we had a difference of opinion and Travis was determined I would see it his way, come hell or high water.

'Anyway!' he said, 'I don't want to talk about it anymore. I am tired now. Let's go to bed.'

I knew his statement meant he was going to want sex and he knew it was never easy for me to have sex when I was not happy. Travis knew he had me over a barrel. He wanted recompense for having to give up his evening and he was going to insist I paid the piper. I was treading a fine line between going to my hen night feeling happy and lighthearted or feeling angry and aggrieved. Even though I didn't want to have sex, I gave in to his demand for a quiet life.

─── CHAPTER TEN ───

IT IS TIME

Time: 10am; 00 hours 00 minutes left to go

Looking at the clock on my bedside table, my heart skipped a beat when I noticed my time was up. Concluding my reflections, I was now clear that I was marrying Travis because I had allowed past beliefs about myself to take hold of my emotional state and dictate my future. Quite simply, I believed I didn't have a choice.

I closed my eyes and was disgusted with myself. For years, I had considered myself a strong woman who knew her mind and would do what was right. Yet, because of my deep-rooted belief that no one would want to marry me, I had remained in a relationship where there was an offer of marriage even though I knew the man wasn't right for me. My desire to experience what it would be like to walk down the aisle and prove everyone wrong, coupled with my fear that I might not get another offer, was the reason I did not decline the proposal of marriage from the beginning. What I should have done was wait to find the right man for me. Instead, here I was about to start preparing to attend my wedding and get married to a man that I really didn't want to marry.

Considering how long we had been together, it sounded ridiculous to say I was sleepwalking through the relationship, but I really believe that was exactly what I was doing. The truth was I didn't think our relationship would last two years let alone ten years. Our moral values and the way we viewed the world had always been the dividing line between us and it was often the cause of many arguments. I believe if someone drops their wallet or purse, if possible, I will alert them to the fact. Travis is completely opposed to my way of thinking. He believes if he was walking behind someone who dropped their wallet, he felt he was under no obligation to let the person know.

This moral difference was something I found difficult to live with from the beginning, yet I did nothing about it. And until today, I didn't believe I was able to do anything about it. Taking control and ending the relationship was always an option and I never took it. It is obvious now, that I saw myself as the victim. There were many occasions during the years when I considered walking away, but I didn't. Because of my belief of not being good enough, the scenario that played out in my mind was that Travis would one day tell me we were done!

Instead, of acting on what my heart and soul was screaming at me to do, I allowed myself to sleepwalk towards the day when I am going to stand in a House of God and say, 'I do!' Without the sugar coating, I had to admit that I was a coward and I was going to pay the price for my cowardice.

Now, that I had faced the reality of my situation, what next? I was about to get married! How could I go through with it? How could I not go through with it? What would other people say? There were so many questions! As these thoughts were being dragged up from the deepest darkest crevices of my being, I realised I had caused the situation I was in by refusing to face the issues niggling at me for a long time. For the second time this morning, lying in my bed reflecting, the old saying came into my mind; *'You've made your bed, now you must lay in it.'*

I threw my legs over the side of the bed and just sat, trying to compose myself, focusing my mind, body and soul. As I stood up and stretched, rotating my head from right to left and then each arm, the anxious feeling began to leave me. A feeling of calm came over me, when I realised that given all of my reflective musings during the last four hours, I had made my decision. I was going to walk down the aisle today and marry Travis!

No longer under any illusion that I was not blameless within the relationship and the victim role I had wrapped myself in had contributed to arriving at this eventful day, left me feeling liberated. I felt empowered to deal with anything that came my way.

Walking towards my wedding dress, still hanging on my bedroom door that had been the anchor used to focus my thinking, I marvelled at the cut of the ivory dress. It was a three piece with a fitted bodice and tiny pearls around the neckline. The skirt was long with an A-line cut and a detachable train. It was lovely and I couldn't wait to put it on! The accessories included: a pearl necklace with matching earrings; a pair of long ivory gloves that would go up past my elbows; a lovely pair of four-inch heel sandals with diamantes across the toe straps; and brand spanking new underwear.

As the train of my wedding dress was detachable, the dress could double for both the wedding and the evening reception. Therefore, there was no need to buy a separate outfit. With regards to the honeymoon, Travis had decided that because we were moving and there was so much to be done to the house we were moving into, the money we had was better used doing the house up the way we wanted it.

Still looking at my dress, I heard Travis' nieces, who were to be my bridesmaids, talking in the spare room they had shared the night before.

'Are you both up?' I called.

'Yes,' they said, 'We are going to get in the shower.'

'Okay!' I responded, 'The woman doing our hair and makeup should be here in a few minutes. I will let her in when she gets here!'

I went into the bathroom, brushed my teeth again and washed my face. As I finished, the doorbell rang. I pulled on my dressing gown, went downstairs and unlocked the front door. To my shock and a little horror because I wasn't sure I completely believed in the 'old wives tale', Travis was at the door.

'Why did you leave the key in the door, I couldn't get in?' he scolded.

'What are you doing here?' I asked a little alarmed. 'The whole point of you sleeping at your brother's house is that it is supposed to be bad luck to see the bride before the wedding!'

'What a load of nonsense,' he challenged. 'I only stayed at Matt's house to shut everyone up because they were all saying the same thing. I had every intention of sneaking back this morning to make sure you were up and everything was going to plan but, you scuppered that by leaving the key in the door. Now, my nieces will know I am here!'

I stood there staring at him with all kinds of thoughts going through my head. This was our wedding day and listen to him! He couldn't even give his berating a rest for one day! He came here to upset me on purpose! He was letting me know who he really was! Otherwise, what reason did he have to want to upset me today? What kind of a person was I marrying? He was letting me know I was trapped! He knew all my family was travelling down for the wedding and that I won't back out now. As my feeling of being empowered slipped away, my only thought was; *'Oh, my God. What have I done?'*

'There is no point standing staring at me. We are getting married today! Is the hairdresser here yet? Where are my nieces, are they up yet?'

I said nothing, I continued to stand and stare, trying to find the courage to end this facade and walk away.

'Come on Melissa,' he urged. 'Cat got your tongue? Get yourself into gear! I have spent a lot of months planning this day and it will go according to my plan.'

I was abruptly pulled from my inaction when the doorbell rang. Travis turned from me and opened the door. It was the hairdresser.

'Hello, you must be Janice, the hairdresser,' Travis said, by way of a greeting. 'I'm Travis, the groom. Come on in, Melissa is ready for you, aren't you darling?' he said, turning to me, 'I know you are probably shocked that I am here,' he continued as he turned back to the hairdresser. 'But I was so anxious to make sure everything went okay and that Melissa didn't get cold feet, I had to come and see if she was alright.'

Janice looked at him with the expression of, 'ah, isn't that sweet' on her face! I felt sick in my stomach.

In that moment, I knew I could not walk away. I would go through with the wedding. Travis had silently called my bluff and had won. I turned to the hairdresser and with a smile, told her I was glad she had arrived early and that my room was upstairs on the left. As she turned to climb the stairs, I looked at Travis and he had a look of triumph on his face.

I turned away from Travis and began to climb the stairs. I had reached the second step when Travis said, 'I don't expect you to keep me waiting at the altar, Melissa. You better get a move on.'

I did not respond. Instead, I kept on climbing. When I was at the top, I plastered a smile on my face and walked towards my bedroom. When I entered, Janice said, 'Ah, it was so nice to see that your fiancé was checking to make sure you were alright. If only my man was so considerate. You are so lucky!'

Instead of responding to her comment, I told her I wanted to have a shower before she started doing my hair. 'No problem,' she said, 'I will use the time to set up and speak with the bridesmaids. By the time, you have finished, I will be ready.'

I escaped to the bathroom and turned on the shower. While the water was running into the bath, I pulled the toilet seat down and sat on it and began to think. When I escaped to the bathroom, I was on the brink of tears. But something had happened to me emotionally between leaving my bedroom, entering the bathroom, and closing the door.

As I sat on the toilet seat, the thoughts I was having didn't feel like mine, they felt alien. It was as if I could feel a steely resolve creeping into my 'usually too close to the surface' emotional state. The feeling of detachment began to take hold. It was almost as if the unfolding events were happening to somebody else. The idea of not being emotionally defeated by Travis was at the forefront of my mind. I could not be one hundred per cent sure, but from his behaviour downstairs, I suspected he thought he had beaten me. What he didn't know was that I was going to survive this because there was no option. And as I wrapped that steely resolve around my heart and my emotions, my spine began to uncurl and I felt myself sitting up straighter on the closed toilet seat. I didn't know where these thoughts were coming from, but I knew I needed them if I was going to get through the wedding and whatever lay beyond.

With a newfound feeling of strength and determination, I showered and left the bathroom ready to have my hair and makeup done. When I re-entered my bedroom, Janice was ready to begin. As I was going to sit down in the chair, she remarked, 'You obviously needed that shower. I didn't want to say anything, but you were looking a bit stressed before you went into the bathroom. Now you look much calmer. It is probably just pre-wedding jitters but don't worry, by the time I finish with your hair and makeup you will feel like a million dollars!'

By the time Janice had done my hair and makeup, I did feel like a million dollars. She had done a great job and I had begun to relax while we were engaging in small talk. When she was done, she suggested I sit and take it easy while she did the hair and makeup for my bridesmaids.

When she left the room, I took her advice. Getting up from the chair I was sitting in, I walked to the window and looked out into the street. The view from my window looked the same as it always did. Only today, the sun was shining. And when it was sunny all the terraced houses on the street looked bright and shiny. Because of the weather, people were leisurely walking past my house, going about their daily business. It amused me – watching the world go by looking the same – but feeling very different. Yet, I knew it was not the world that was different, it was me. I was on the cusp of plunging into a life-changing event and yet the planet continued to turn as usual.

While standing at the window looking at the outside world, I began to redefine what my life was going to be in the future. In less than two hours, I was going to be married to Travis and to quote the adage of; 'start as you mean to carry on.' I had decided that – going forward – there would be a different Melissa. I knew that from this day forward, I was no longer going to accept any of Travis' crap. Standing up for myself was going to be the way I functioned. I knew I was made of stronger stuff even though I had allowed myself to be manipulated and my strength of character to be diminished.

When I had started my reflections in the early hours of the morning, I had begun by blaming Travis for being manipulative and trying to control me, but in all honesty, I had allowed myself to be manipulated and given him permission to have the upper hand. I was in no doubt that my change in behaviour was going to be hard on Travis and he might not accept the new me. For my own sanity and emotional wellbeing, however, this was a risk I was prepared to take. It was at this point that

I had another revelation. Travis and I had never been able to communicate on that deeper level that addresses the emotional thoughts and feelings considered so important in promoting a healthy relationship.

If I tried to drill down into issues that were too deep, he accused me of 'overthinking' everything. What I now realised was that this was his way of preventing me from unpicking his thoughts and not thinking too deeply about his moral values, which we always disagreed about. We looked at life in completely different ways and because of the contention it always caused between us, I shied away from it. This had to change in the future.

'Come in,' I responded to a tap on the bedroom door. My maid of honour, Simone popped her head around the door.

'Ah! Here is the bride to be! Am I too early to help you get dressed? I want to make sure you look perfect.'

I looked at my watch and I couldn't believe how long I had been standing at the window.

'Come in, Simone,' I said, 'You look lovely and I am glad you are here. Have you checked on my bridesmaids?'

'Yes!' she responded. 'They are dressed and waiting for you to get ready.'

'Okay!' I said. 'My hair and face have been done, so let's get my dress on.'

'Are you alright?' Simone asked.

I was taken off guard by the question because I thought I had done a good job in making sure none of my thoughts were present on my face or in my body language. 'I am fine, why do you ask?'

'Oh, I don't know,' she said, 'You look kind of different. Are you sure you are okay?'

To appease her, I said, 'You are married and you know what it is like. I got up this morning and I was feeling a little apprehensive. I gave myself a good talking to, got myself in hand and I feel fine now.'

Simone gave me a long hard look but didn't say anything and I wasn't sure if she believed me.

'Come on then,' she said, 'Let's get you dressed.'

Starting with my underwear, we carefully added each layer until I was completely dressed. When I looked in the mirror, I had to admit I looked stunning. For a second, a feeling of sadness overcame me when I thought it was a pity I was getting married to a man I did not think I was going to spend the rest of my life with.

Simone had been downstairs answering the front door because the photographer, florist, my brother, who was giving me away, and my mother had arrived. When she walked back into my bedroom, I was standing in front of the full-length mirror and she said, 'You look lovely Melissa,' as she walked up behind me and looked at my reflection in the mirror. She then turned me around and looked directly at me.

'I know there is something going on in that head of yours,' she said. 'But remember you are marrying somebody that absolutely adores you and I have no doubt you will be really happy. Let's get you down that aisle!'

We walked towards the bedroom door and Simone opened it for me. Before we stepped through into the hallway, she positioned my train so it was trailing behind me. She handed me my bouquet of flowers and as she did so, I looked over my right shoulder and said, 'Travis was here this morning!'

'What! Why?' she exclaimed. 'Doesn't he know it is bad luck?'

I didn't answer her. While she was getting her head around what I had said and what I was implying, I left my bedroom and made my way to the top of the stairs. When I looked down, my mother, brother, bridesmaids and the photographer were standing waiting for me. Everyone was smiling up at me and saying lots of 'Ohs' and 'Ahs' and the photographer started taking pictures.

I knew Simone wanted to ask me why Travis had been at the house this morning but she didn't have the chance. The wedding cars had arrived and there was lots of milling around as everyone was admiring my dress and getting ready to leave the house and travel to the church.

When I walked out of the house, the wedding cars were lined up and waiting for everyone to climb in. When I got into the back of the Bentley, I looked back at the house and the street and thought, **here we go, Melissa**.

The day had turned out to be sunny and very hot and as we travelled towards the church, everything looked bright and sparkling. When the Bentley pulled up in front of the church, there were a lot of people standing outside. My arrival signaled it was time to enter the church. This gave me a few minutes to gather my thoughts. My brother must have known I needed a minute because he sat quietly beside me.

'Are you ready?' he asked me after a few minutes had ticked by. I looked at him and nodded without saying a word. My brother stepped out of his side of the car and walked around to my door. He opened it and I took his arm. As we entered the church, ahead of my maid of honour and bridesmaids, I knew my decision to go through with this wedding was not one of my better decisions, but the deed was done and whatever came next, I would deal with it.

As I stood in the church vestibule waiting for the organist to cue me in, I was surprised at how calm I felt. The organist started playing the music Travis had selected for my walk down the aisle.

My bother turned to me again.

'Are you ready?' he asked.

When I nodded, he placed my left hand on his right arm and we began to proceed down the aisle. As I looked up, there was Travis standing next to his best man looking very much like the adoring groom. Without turning my head – relying instead on my peripheral vision – I took in the facial expressions of the church guests as I walked past them. Even though I felt like a fraud and a liar for deceiving our wedding guests into believing this was a match made in heaven, I was glad I was no longer deceiving myself.

Digging deep to recover the steely resolve I needed, I plastered a smile on my face and continued walking towards the man I was going to marry and an uncertain future.

ABOUT THE AUTHOR

Marcia was born in Bristol, in the South West of England, but grew up in the Midlands. After qualifying as a social worker from Derby University in 1994, Marcia moved to London to live with her partner who she married and had a son with.

As a child, Marcia could not think of anything better than getting lost in the pages of a fiction novel when she was not meeting up with friends. She had always dreamt that one day she would have the confidence to write her own books based on themes that were true to life.

Her dream of becoming a writer, however, was postponed as the demands of being a wife, mother and working full-time, as well as managing the curve balls life can sometimes throw in our way, were the primary focus.

Learning from some of life's most challenging experiences and wanting to share her learning, reignited the pull to write her own books. Now divorced – with a grown-up son – Marcia finally plucked up the courage to realise her dream and write the first of *The Mental Gymnastics* series, a trilogy.

By sharing this story with the world, Marcia hopes to help other people who have been in similar situations.

Lightning Source UK Ltd.
Milton Keynes UK
UKHW02f2157211117
313110UK00004B/26/P